Casualties of War

By
Arlene & Ali Brathwaite

BRATHWAITE PUBLISHING
www.brathwaitepublishing.com

Books by Arlene & Ali Brathwaite are published by
Brathwaite Publishing
P.O. Box 38205
Albany, New York 12203

Copyright © 2012 by Arlene Brathwaite
Library of Congress Number:
ISBN: (13 Digit) # 978-0-9797462-9-1

This book was printed in the United States of America.

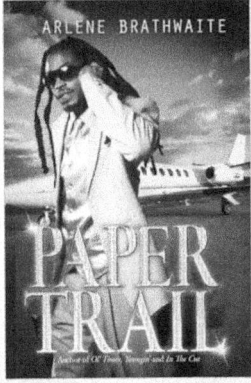

ACKNOWLEDGMENTS

An author's success is never the result of just their dedication and hard work. It is the consorted effort of the many men and women working behind the scenes who are just as dedicated and hard working.

Brathwaite Publishing continues to grow because of its team of talented professionals and our commitment to readers all over the world who have come to expect nothing but our best.

Special thanks go out to our content editors Candace Caldwell and Andrea Anthony; and to our proofreaders Shavina Richardson and Leslie Michelle. Thank you for your honesty and constructive criticism.

A special thanks to the actors who participated in the book trailer for Casualties of War: Melissa Inynn, Carlos Garcia, Tenesha Smith, Curtis Witters, Quavon "Keylo Red" Page, Shataya Scott, Levonne Williams, Haseim Townsend, Michael Doraby, and Erica Johnson.

We have to give Craig "Real Love" Henry a paragraph by himself, because he has been an invaluable asset to us. He ran the day-to-day operations of our bookstore (The Book Club, Albany, NY) when we had to take the time off to finish Casualties of War. He's not just our employee, he's family, and we are blessed to have him in our lives.

And last but not least, thank you to all the supporters of Brathwaite Publishing. You are the engine of this machine. You drive us to give you nothing but the best.

CHAPTER 1

Ten pm, Middle Eastern time, three shadows entered a desolate Iraqi town that had been hammered by Marines in heavily-armored Humvees earlier that day. The shadows halted at the mouth of an alleyway. Sewers, destroyed in the earlier bombardment, overflowed filling the streets with human excrement, blanketing the air with a stinging stench. Shattered glass, splintered wood, and twisted metal littered the streets like ticker tape after a parade.

With just a sliver of light from the new moon, the skeleton crew zigzagged their way through the cluttered alleyway with ease. Coming out from the other side of the alleyway, their eyes picked out the brick dwelling their target was supposed to be. The team leader flashed a hand signal at his team, indicating that they should keep their eyes open. Their identities were concealed behind greasepaint and black fatigues. The Iraqis who dared to speak of the American special ops team referred to them as "the demons" because they would come in the folds of the night and snatch up suspected insurgents who would never be seen or heard from again.

Tonight the demons were after Zakawi. He and his band of rebels attacked an army maintenance convoy killing every soldier. The demons sprinted single file alongside charred cars and trucks then separated when they reached the house. Demons

One and Two took up positions on either side of the front door while Demon Three posted up at the backdoor.

According to reliable Intel, Zakawi lived here with his wife and mother. The mission was simple: snatch up Zakawi and hang his mutilated body from a streetlight for all to see. Demon One clicked the TALK button on his radio, signaling that they were going in, in five, four, three, two… Demons One and Two kicked in the front door while Demon Three kicked in the back. They zipped in and out of the rooms, M-4 rifles leading the way. Demon Three posted up in the living room while Demons One and Two continued searching through the small dwelling. Moments later, Demons One and Two shoved Zakawi's wife and mother into the living room. Demon One looked at Demon Three and shook his head, signaling that Zakawi wasn't in the house.

"Quiet!" Demon One said to the two women in Arabic. The women muffled their sobs and kept their eyes to the floor. Demon One nudged Zakawi's wife with his boot. "Where's your husband?"

"I don't know," she quickly responded. Demon One dragged her by her hair, away from Zakawi's mother, and slammed her to the floor and planted his boot on the back of her neck. "I swear I don't know where he is," she choked out. "He left this morning and he hasn't returned."

Demon Three caught movement at the back porch and ran to the back of the house while unsheathing a commando knife. As soon as the figure stepped through the backdoor, Demon Three kicked the person in the stomach. Demon Three pulled off the head cover and realized that the person was a girl no older than seventeen. The girl opened her mouth to scream but Demon Three clamped her hand over the girl's mouth while resting the knife blade on the girl's cheek. "You make a sound, and I'll cut out your tongue." Demon Three threatened in fluid Arabic.

The girl stopped breathing.

"Who are you?" Demon Three asked.

"I am Jamilah."

"Why are you here?"

"I live here."

"Who are you to Zakawi?"

Jamilah's lips quivered. "I am his daughter."

Demon Three gasped. Intel said nothing of a daughter.

"Please don't kill me; I love America," Jamilah whispered.

Demon Three cut off two strips of cloth from Jamilah's head covering and tied Jamilah's hands behind her back and marched her into the living room. Jamilah saw her mother on the floor fighting for air as a strange man had his boot on the back of her neck. Jamilah tried running to her, but Demon Three snatched her by her hair and forced her to her knees. Demon One looked at Jamilah.

"Zakawi's daughter," Demon Three said.

"Really?"

Zakawi's wife struggled to speak. "Please... don't hurt her."

Demon One took his boot off her neck. Before she had a chance to run to her daughter, Demon Two slipped his arms under her armpits and locked her into a full nelson.

Demon One grabbed Jamilah and threw her to the floor on her and started ripping off her dress. Zakawi's wife struggled against Demon Two's hold, but she could do nothing but watch Jamilah being stripped. Zakawi's mother tried to scuttle toward Jamilah but was stopped with a boot to the head by Demon Three.

Demon One jammed his boot against Jamilah's neck and then looked at Zakawi's wife. "Where is he?"

"Please, I don't know." Demon One looked at Demon Three. "Chair." Demon Three didn't budge. "I said chair!"

Demon Three grabbed the wooden chair and broke off a leg and tossed it to him. Demon One twirled it a few times then positioned the splintered end on Jamilah's soft opening. He looked a Zakawi's wife with a smirk.

"Last chance."

Zakawi's wife became hysterical and almost broke free from Demon Two's hold, but he quickly sank it back in so she couldn't move.

"So be it," Demon One said.

"Our orders were specific," Demon Three said.

"Things have changed; we have to improvise," Demon One responded.

"This is bullshit. They don't know anything."

"And how would you know that?" Demon One questioned.

"They would've talked by now," Demon Two responded.

Demon One sneered. "Well, being that they don't want to talk, I want to hear them scream."

Demon Three drew her sidearm.

"What the fuck are you doing?" Demon One asked.

"What the fuck are *you* doing?" Demon Three responded.

"Holster your weapon."

Demon Two cut his eyes at his watch. "We don't have time for this."

"Drop the chair leg," Demon Three said to Demon One.

"And if I don't?"

Demon Three walked toward him. When she got within striking distance, she kicked him in the chest, landing him on his ass; then holstered her gun.

Demon One slowly got back to his feet. "You got a lot of shit with you." And with that, he rushed her. They crashed to the floor and rolled around, each trying to outmaneuver the other.

Demon One got on top of Demon Three and punched her in the face. She blocked the next blow and threw two of her own that backed Demon One off her. They both sprung to their feet ready to go at it again.

"Look out!" Demon Two yelled. Jamilah had worked her hands free and had picked up the chair leg. She charged Demon One from behind.

"Die America!" She flung the chair leg with all her might.

Demon One leaned to the left. Demon Three saw the projectile too late. The splintered end pierced her throat. Without thinking she pulled it out. Blood sprayed out of the wound like a geyser. Before passing out, she saw Demon One shove Jamilah to the ground and stomped on her head until she stopped moving. Then she heard two gunshots. She knew Zakawi's wife and mother and had just been executed.

Demon Two started applying pressure to Demon Three's wound. "She's losing a lot of blood." He froze when he saw a line of headlights in the distance bouncing toward the house. Demon One tapped him on the shoulder.

"Strip her. We can't do anything for her."

"Sir—"

"I said strip her; we've got to go now."

Demon Two stripped Demon Three of her weapons and communications equipment. They slipped out the back and disappeared into the night.

Three years later...

Omar sat on the edge of the bed smoking a cigarette. Myra watched his wide back expand and contract as he pulled on the Newport and blew out a cloud of smoke. She scratched the back of her neck, allowing him to saturate his lungs with nicotine before she spoke.

"We cool?" she said.

Omar grabbed his jeans off the floor and slid them on; then pulled out a bag of heroin from his front pocket and tossed it over his shoulder.

Myra snatched it out the air before it had a chance to hit the bed. "Thank you," she whispered. "I was thinking... if you ever need me to hold onto something like I did last time—"

"Last time you weren't a fiend."

"I'm not a dope fiend."

"I like you, Myra. I would hate to have to kill you over a couple bags of dope."

"I would never steal from you."

"And three months ago you told me you would never fuck me for a bag of dope."

Myra bowed her head.

Omar pulled on his shirt and faced her. "Hey, I didn't mean it like that."

"No you're right; only a dope fiend would prostitute her body for a bag of dope."

Omar looked down at her body. Myra wasn't the traditional bony, Barbie doll beauty plastered all over the billboards and magazine covers. She was cleanly shaven—no hair on her head, arms, legs, or pubic area. And although she had been shooting and snorting heroin for six months, her body still retained its sculpted edge. Her skin was smooth to the eye, yet firm to the touch. Blemishes were camouflaged by her mocha complexion. The only mark her melanin couldn't conceal was the ragged scar that ran across her neck. An attention grabber she expertly concealed with bandanas, scarfs, and turtlenecks.

Omar cupped her chin and coaxed her to look at him. "Hey, look on the bright side; I know a lot of dudes who would give you a couple bags just to sniff your ass."

"Thanks. You really know how to make a woman feel good about herself."

"I'm out," Omar said. He snapped his fingers at Myra when he noticed that she was too focused on the bag in her hand to hear him. "Hey, I'm talking to you."

"huh?"

"I said I'm leaving."

"You may not believe me but I would never sleep with anyone else; I don't care how many bags they offered."

Omar crawled back on the bed and pecked her on the lips. "If I ever find out that you're messing with any of these lowlifes, it's over between me and you. You'll be paying for your fix like everybody else. Which reminds me—"

"My check will be here tomorrow; I'll have your money." Myra got off the bed and walked him to the door. She locked it behind him and hustled back to her bedroom. She dumped the bag of heroin onto the dresser and made four lines. She snorted the lines one after the other and then crawled back into the bed.

She touched the scar on her neck and then let her hand fall to her side. Her eyes drooped as a blissful feeling warmed every part of her body.

"Fuck you," she mumbled to the demons in her past that left her for dead. "Motherfuck all of you."

Myra jumped out of her sleep. She lay sprawled across her bed. She slowly sat up and reached for her pack of Newports. Her jaw tightened when she flipped open the top and only saw two in the box she just opened last night. She pictured Omar sneaking into her room last night and grabbing a handful of cigarettes out the pack. *All the dope money he's making and he can't buy a pack of cigarettes.* She lit one up and took a long pull. She rolled her eyes and sighed as her cellphone rang. Whoever it was refused to leave a message and kept calling right back. Myra tried to ignore the caller as she grabbed a pair of sweatpants off the floor and a tank top she spotted hanging on her bedpost. A few seconds later, her phone rang again.

She snatched it off the dresser. "What!"

"Myra, are you okay?" the caller asked.

"No, Doc, I'm not okay. You're calling me like every two seconds. You're driving me crazy."

"Well, you missed you're ten o' clock appointment this morning. I was worried about you."

"My meetings are on Wednesdays, Doc."

"Today is Wednesday."

If Myra had to guess what day it was, she would have guessed it was Monday because she couldn't remember anything after Sunday afternoon. "Forgive me, Doc. I've been having a rough week."

"I guess asking you to come in today would be out of the question."

"Maybe tomorrow or—"

"Tomorrow's fine. Are you still taking your meds?" Dr. Randal asked, referring to the antidepressants she prescribed for Myra.

Myra looked at her dresser draw full of pill bottles. "Just refilled the prescription yesterday."

"How are you feeling?"

"Not feeling too much of anything these days."

"I'm putting you down for one o' clock tomorrow afternoon. You *need* to show up, Myra."

That was Dr. Randal's way of saying that if she didn't show, she was going to report her no shows to the army psychologists overseeing her treatment. That meant that the army would put a hold on her disability check until someone paid her a visit and got to the bottom of why she wasn't attending her mandated sessions with her civilian psychiatrist.

"I'll be there, Doc." Myra ended the call and headed downstairs to the mailboxes. She unlocked hers and there was her check begging for her to rip it open and cash it. Her thoughts began to race as she thought about all the dope she was going to have in her hands in a few hours. She called Omar on her way to the check cashing spot.

"What up?" Omar said, as he answered his phone.

"I need you to come through," Myra said.

"You got your check?"

"On my way to cash it now."

"How much you looking for?"

"A bundle."

"I'll be there in half an hour." Omar ended the call. "Hurry up and eat that shit, we out," he said to his man, Moon, as he prepared to leave the fish and chips spot.

"Who was that?" Moon asked, as he continued stuffing his face with french-fries. When Omar didn't respond, Moon looked up from his plate and saw Omar staring toward the entrance.

"Oh shit," Omar said.

"I knew I would find you here," a man from Omar's past said.

"Motherfucking Emmit the Vietnamese rockstar. I haven't seen you since high school. Last I heard, you and your band of punk rockers were touring in the UK."

"I gave that up. I used that gig to travel, get high, and get chicks."

"And why would you want to give that up?"

"It was time for me to grow up and start making some real money."

"I see," Omar said, eyeing Emmit's Kenneth Cole suit and square-toed shoes.

"What up, E?" Moon said, as he pushed his plate away from himself.

Emmit bumped his fist against Moon's. "I'm just living the life."

"What's really good?" Omar asked. "I know you didn't stake out my favorite take-out spot just to catch up on old times."

Emmit pulled out a chair and sat at the table. "I'm in town for a few days on business."

"Business?" Omar stroked his goatee as his criminal mind kicked into greezy mode.

"An associate of mine needs to cop some weight in order to facilitate a business deal he's got going on. So, I figured I'd slide some business your way and maybe get a package deal."

"How much is your associate looking to cop?"

"Two squares."

Omar busted out laughing. "Yo, E, you's a funny dude." I forgot how you used to clown around 'n' shit."

"Do I look like I'm clowning, O?"

Omar peeped the diamond encrusted Rolex peeking from under Emmit's shirt cuff and the pinky ring that looked like it cost more than every piece of jewelry Omar had on.

"Okay," Omar said. "How soon can you get up the 30G's?"

"Yesterday."

Omar laughed again. "Motherfucking Emmit. You really are living the life, huh?"

"We only have one life to live."

Omar's phone chirped. He looked at the caller ID.

"Business?" Emmit asked.

"I have to be somewhere in ten minutes."

"Well, don't let me stop you. Here's my number." He scribbled it on a napkin and handed it to Omar. "Give me a call tomorrow afternoon and we'll discuss the details."

"I'll do that." Omar tucked the napkin in his pocket. He watched Emmit leave and then looked at Moon. "What do you think?"

"Fuck that ponytail-down-the-back wearing Chinese motherfucker."

"He's Vietnamese."

"Whatever. I never trusted that slanted eye faggot." Moon pulled his food back in front of himself. "So, you think he's for real?"

"If he's wasting my time, you'll have a reason to kill him."

"I'll don't need a reason to kill that faggot."

Omar stood up. "We out; we can finish this conversation on the way to Myra's."

Myra rushed to the door when she heard Omar's familiar knock. She cracked the door and barely got out the way before Omar and Moon pushed past her. She immediately regretted answering the door in just an oversized T-shirt. She thought Omar was going to hand her the bundle, grab his money, and leave. She wasn't expecting him to make himself comfortable on her living room couch, and she definitely didn't expect Moon to be helping himself to what was in her refrigerator.

"What's up, Moon?" she asked angrily.

"What's up with you doing some food shopping? I got more food in my stomach than you do in your fridge."

Myra planted her hands on her hips. "You got more food in that big ass stomach than every fridge in this building."

Moon tried to slam the fridge door, but his stomach got in the way. Omar busted out laughing.

"Come here," he said to Myra.

"I got your money."

"Did I ask for my money? I said come here."

Myra took a few steps and stopped when Omar rubbed his crotch.

"Look, Omar—"

"I said come here!" He snatched her by the wrist and pulled her onto his lap. "You wanna act all brand new on me 'cause Moon's here."

"I just want to give you your money."

"And?"

"And get what you're supposed to have for me."

"Yeah, I have something for you," Omar said, while running his hand up and down her calf.

"Omar, please."

"Please what?" He raised her shirt above her thigh.

Myra pulled it back down. She heard Moon's heavy breathing and turned to look at him. He was munching on a box of Cheez-Its he found in the cabinet.

"Don't mind me. Make believe I'm not even here."

Myra jumped when Omar pinched her nipple. She squirmed out of his grip and climbed off him. She folded her arms and shot him a wicked look.

"Damn, I'm just fucking with you." Omar stood up. "Go get my money so I can get the fuck out of here."

Myra went to her room and came back with a handful of cash. Omar pocketed it and handed her a bundle.

"Don't hit it all at once." Omar snickered and then turned to Moon. "We out."

Moon closed the box of Cheez-Its and tucked it under his arm. He stared at Myra like he wanted to pour a bottle of hot sauce all over her and eat her up. She looked at the floor as he walked past her. She locked the door behind them and raced to her bedroom.

Tears flowed as she fought to calm herself. Omar had no idea how close he came to having his neck snapped like a twig. And Moon... Myra would have toyed with him before ending his miserable existence. She emptied a bag of dope onto her dresser and made two lines. She snorted the lines and stood still for a minute.

Myra didn't realize how messed up in the head she really was until she came back from the Middle East. She knew Afghanistan, Iraq, Pakistan, and Yemen better than the five boroughs. She spoke Afghan, Arabic, Persian, Punjabi, and Urdu better than most of the indigenous people of those countries. She went through months of debriefing when she returned to the States. But all the army did was strip away all the identities she had become in order to fight the war on terror in the terrorists' own backyard. Her toughest mission, by far, was putting the war behind her and living a normal life. For Myra Taft, there was no such thing as normal. Dr. Randal wrote her prescriptions for anxiety and depression, but the atrocities Myra carried out and witnessed in those desert lands couldn't be suppressed with a pill and a glass of water. That's when she turned to drinking at the local bar and met Omar.

Omar had been the first civilian she spoke to when she was discharged from the army. He found her intriguing, with her baldhead, pretty face, and reserved demeanor. It took him a few nights of delicate prodding, but he finally got her to open up. She admitted that she hated the taste of beer and that she didn't like the hangovers she got after drinking hard liquor. Omar's predatory mind kicked in. It was obvious Myra was going through something and was trying to battle it with alcohol. He offered her a better alternative, heroin. It was the perfect solution for her... and him. Whatever problems she was battling wouldn't stand a chance against the White Night (his brand of heroin). And her addiction would make it that much easier for him to get in her pants. To Omar's surprise, Myra accepted the dope. Four weeks later, she was a slave to the White Night and Omar was jousting her with his lance.

Myra opened another bag and made two more lines on her dresser. She snorted them and flopped back on her bed. She didn't want to kill Omar and Moon anymore. *Can't kill them. If I bring any attention to myself, they'll send the demons after me. Can't have that now, can we?*

Myra showed up for her one o'clock appointment ten minutes early. Instead of taking the elevator, she opted to sprint up the four flights of stairs. She arrived on the fourth floor quicker than the elevator would have and she was barely breathing hard. She stepped out of the stairwell and almost bumped into Dr. Randal.

"You're early," Dr. Randal said, switching her coffee from one hand to the other to look at her watch.

"I figured the quicker I get in, the quicker I'll get out."

"We'll see about that." Dr. Randal led her past the double doors and into her office. "Make yourself comfortable." Dr. Randal's office was spacious and stylish. It was furnished with stained-wood tables with black leather chairs. The wall behind her desk displayed her credentials and various awards and plaques she'd already acquired in her three-year career.

Myra felt a sense of pride seeing a young black woman excelling in the field of psychiatry the way Dr. Laura Randal had. Today, Laura let her curly locks dangle around the frame of her baby face.

Myra walked past *the couch* and sat in a straight-back chair. She had no intentions of ever lying on a couch and talking about shit that happened to her when she was five-years-old.

Laura sat down and crossed her legs. "How are you doing today?"

"No pen and pad today, Doc?"

"Not today. Maybe we can just talk, off the record."

"What do you want to talk about?" Myra asked.

"I'll let you decide."

Myra sat forward in the chair. "I want to talk about me getting these sessions cut down to once a month, because this is a waste of time for the both of us."

"I understand that the army made seeing a civilian psychiatrist mandatory, but they allowed you to choose which psychiatrist you wanted to see and you chose me. Now I can't force you to open up, but the longer you keep this wall up, the harder it is going to be for you to knock it down."

"I'm fine, Doc."

"I hardly call living with Post-Traumatic Stress Disorder fine. I'm not going to lie to you and tell you that I can feel your pain—"

"Pain? I wish that was all I was feeling. Try betrayal. I fought for my country, risked my life, and what do I get? A disability check and mandated meetings with a shrink barely out of college. What are you, twenty-four?"

"Twenty-six."

"This is bullshit and you know it."

"What's bullshit?" Laura asked.

"Come on, Doc, don't insult my intelligence. You didn't get all of those plaques for your good looks. So, let's just drop the charade. All I have to do is show up and stare at your ugly mug for an hour."

"True, you can stare at me for an hour, but you're more fucked up in the head than I thought if you think I'm an ugly mug; I'm far from that."

Myra tried to keep a straight face, but seeing Laura snake her neck and drop her prissy persona brought a smile to her face.

"Don't let the awards and plaques fool you."

"And what's that supposed to mean?" Myra asked.

"Now, who's insulting whose intelligence?" Laura took a sip of her coffee. "I tell you what, I'll start." She started to recite Myra's file from memory. "Specialist Myra Taft, U.S. Army. Most recent tour was in Iraq. You were the only woman in a unit of forty-five soldiers. You operated a retransmission station in the mountains of Northern Iraq and then in the center of Baghdad."

"I'm impressed, Doc."

"How did it feel to be the only woman in your unit?"

"Uncomfortable, to say the least. We shared the same toilet, slept in the same quarters…"

"Did any of the soldiers ever try to come on to you?"

"Of course. I was able to turn many of them away with a firm get-the-fuck-out-of-my-face look, but then there were some who I knew would gang rape me if the opportunity ever arose."

"How did you feel with them?"

Myra ran her hand over her scalp. "I shaved my head and became the bitch from hell."

"And how did that work?"

"They went from wanting to rape me to wanting to kill me, so I think it worked out pretty well."

Laura smiled. "You were a gutsy woman."

"I wasn't a woman. I was a soldier. I didn't have the luxury of being a woman."

"What about now?"

"Are you kidding? Can you picture me with my hair and nails done?"

"Yes; and I can see you wearing a dress with a pair of Gucci sandals and a Gucci handbag to match."

"If you can see that, then *you're* more fucked up in the head than I thought."

Both women laughed.

Laura then spoke softly. "What did you mean by betrayal? Does it have anything to do with you being taken hostage?"

"I don't want to talk about it."

"Your unit was ambushed. Everyone in your unit was killed except you. It took the army a few weeks to find you, but they did. Do you believe someone gave your unit's location to the insurgents?"

Myra wanted to grab Laura by her shoulders and shake her. She wanted to tell her what happened, what really happened. She wanted, no, she *needed* to, but she couldn't. "Let it go, Doc."

"I'm just trying to help."

"I don't remember asking for your help. I just want to be left alone. I'm trying to have some semblance of a life, but it's hard when someone's constantly pulling the scab off a wound that hasn't fully healed. After a while, tearing off the scab becomes more painful than the wound itself."

Laura nodded. "You're right. I'll make a deal with you. From now on, you can come to all of our sessions and stare at me for the whole hour if you like. I'll sign off on all your evaluations and even cut your sessions down to once every two weeks. All I ask is if you ever feel the need to talk, you call me. Deal?"

"Six months into this thing and I think we're finally starting to make some progress, Doc."

Laura retrieved one of her business cards off her desk and wrote her home number on the back. "Call me anytime, you hear me?"

Myra took the card from her and slipped it in her back pocket. "See you in two weeks, Doc."

CHAPTER 2

O mar sat on the stoop of his building enjoying one of the few days out of the summer it wasn't raining. Women paraded back and forth past his stoop, pretending to be playing with their kids, but Omar could tell by the way these mothers were swinging and twisting their bodies that they were just waiting for him to invite them upstairs to play house.

Omar was dressed in lax mode, Stacy Adams sandals, Calvin Klein slacks, and a G-unit tank top. He was never the heavy-wearing jewelry type, but he wanted the lowlifes to know he was caking like Pillsbury; so his symbol of getting money was the diamond and platinum Gucci chain he donned like the crown jewels.

The streetlights started to flicker, alerting the grownups and kids that the day and its sunlight were giving way to the night and it nocturnal predators. A cab pulled up to the curb and out stepped Emmit wearing another designer suit and a pair of Italian shoes. He pulled off his yellow-tinted shades and extended his hand. "I was beginning to think you weren't going to call."

"I had some business to take care of," Omar lied, as he shook his hand. Omar peeped the brown-skinned beauty sitting in the backseat of the cab staring at him. He could only see her upper body, but her bare shoulders told him she was wearing a strapless dress. A dress that was no doubt just as expensive as Emmit's suit. Omar nodded at her. She looked away, obviously upset about something.

"Don't mind her," Emmit said, watching the whole exchange take place. "We're on our way to a musical and she doesn't like to be late."

"We could've discussed this over the phone and saved you the trip."

"Nah," Emmit said, sitting down next to him. "I like to conduct business face to face."

"So, let's talk business."

Emmit cupped his fist with his hand and spoke, "I'm going to be straight up with you, we go too far back for me to bullshit you."

Omar snorted. Most liars always started with saying that they're going to be honest. "I'm listening."

"This guy I'm working for is willing to throw a lot of business your way if your product is good."

"You know my shit is of the highest quality."

"True that. I just want to make sure that you know that he's expecting the best. The better, the more he cops, the more money I make, feel me?"

"Just have my money ready tomorrow night. I'll call you around seven with the address."

Emmit stood up and tinkered with his cufflink. "I'll be waiting for your call. And O, it's great seeing you again."

Omar winked. "Good seeing you, too."

Emmit climbed back into the cab and waved at Omar as it pulled off.

"We still on?" Shelly asked Emmit, as she interlaced her fingers with his.

"Everything's a go."

"You should've set the deal up for five kilos," K-Long, the pretend cab driver said.

"He would've definitely known something was up. Two is enough for us to set up shop." Emmit squeezed Shelly's hand. "Contact your friend in Syracuse and let him know we'll be up there by the end of the week."

Shelly nodded. "And you're sure your friend doesn't suspect anything?"

"Omar's bitch-ass ain't going to know what hit him."

"Shit!" Omar gritted his teeth as he unloaded into the hot mom he invited up to his place to play house. "I see why you have five kids, Marcella." He tried to pull out of her, but she kept her legs wrapped around his waist.

Omar's cell chirped. "He pulled out of her and rolled onto his back. "What up?"

"How'd the meet with Emmit go?" Moon asked.

"We're on for tomorrow night."

Moon didn't say anything.

"What?" Omar said.

"I don't trust that motherfucker."

"He's legit. You saw the way he was dressed at the fish spot. And he was dressed the same way today, and he had a bitch with him. They were on their way to a musical

Moon sighed. "I don't know, O, he just rubs me the wrong way."

Omar looked down at Marcella as she tugged the used condom off him. She looked up at him with a devilish grin and then took him in her mouth.

"So, you're saying we shouldn't mess with him?"

"Until we know he's for real, I say we do the first couple deals somewhere other than the stash house."

"So where do you suggest we deal?"

"I don't know." Moon thought for a moment. "Let's do it at Myra's."

"Yeah, yeah, whatever." Omar steadied his breathing as Marcella took him to the back of her throat. "I'll catch up with you in the morning." He ended the call and watched Marcella as she went to work on him. "You're going to mess around and make me marry you."

Myra sat at her wobbly kitchen table staring at her last three bags of dope. *Shit I just copped this bundle from Omar last night. It hasn't even been a full twenty-four hours and I already went through seventeen bags.* She opened a pack of Newports and pulled out a cigarette. She bit down on the cotton filter and pulled it out with her teeth and then crushed it into a ball before sitting it into the cooker. She dumped the three bags of dope into her cooker and then drew up 20 milligrams of water into her syringe and squirted it into the cooker. She then grabbed her lighter, lit the bottom of her cooker, and watched the dope dissolve. She placed the cooker on the table and tied her belt around her arm.

Myra started humming as she drew the cloudy liquid into the syringe. "Here we go." She plucked the syringe to get the bubbles out and then stuck the needle into her vein and injected the White knight into her blood stream.

"White Knight," she chuckled. "My knight in shining armor; in this case, in a shiny needle." Her eyes drooped as the White knight galloped through her bloodstream. "Charge! High-ho Silver! Up, up and away!" She giggled.

Over the months, Myra could feel her senses dimming, her reflexes dulling, but she didn't care, as long as she knew she could still kick half the world's ass. "Shit." She realized the needle was still in her arm. She pulled it out and loosened the belt from around her arm. "Motherfucking dope. I swear, I would hate you if I didn't love you so much."

Myra jumped up, almost flipping the rickety kitchen table when she heard the bomb blasts. She looked around disorientated. "What the—" The bomb blasts went off again followed by a muffled voice. "Myra, open the fucking door."

"Omar?" Myra shuffled to the door and opened it. "Omar, what are you doing—"

"I've been trying to reach you all day," Omar said, as he pushed past her. Moon followed in behind him. "I thought you O.D'd or something."

Myra held the door open. "Now's not a good time. I just woke up."

"Fuck all that," Omar said. "I need you to get lost for two hours."

"Two hours? What the hell is going on?"

"I have someone coming through to pick something up."

Myra's eyes widened. "Pick something up at my place? No. Hell no."

"Hey, don't I look out for you? You said if I ever needed you to hold onto something—"

"Hold, Omar. I said hold. That doesn't mean you can start selling dope out of my apartment." Myra spun when she heard her TV come on. "Hey." She ran up on Moon, who had made himself comfortable on the couch, and snatched the remote out of his hand. "This is not happening." She turned to Omar. "This is not happening."

"Myra," Omar cooed, as he walked up to her and put his arm around her waist. "I'm sorry, baby, I didn't mean to just barge in here and get you all riled up." He pulled her to him. "I really need you right now."

"Omar, I can't let you sell drugs out of my apartment."

"Just this one time, baby. I'll swear on a stack of Bibles if you want me to, just this one deal. This guy is walking in and walking right out."

"Omar—"

He put a finger to her lips. "Shh." He pulled out a bundle from his jacket

pocket, placed it in the palm of her hand, and then closed her fingers around it. "To show my appreciation."

Myra looked down at her hand and then looked up at him. "Give me your word that this will be the first and last time you sell anything out of my place."

Omar looked her in the eyes. "You have my word."

Myra pulled away from him. "I'm not going anywhere for two hours. I'll be in my room. Do this deal and then get the fuck out of my house." Myra stormed off to the bathroom and slammed the door.

"That bitch is crazy," Moon said.

"This was your idea, remember?"

"Whatever. Turn the TV on," Moon said.

"Get off your fat ass and turn it on yourself." Omar pulled out his phone and made the call.

Emmit just stepped out of the motel shower when his cell rang. He wrapped a towel around his waist and picked his phone off the sink's ledge. He smiled when he saw Omar's number on the caller ID. "What's good, O?"

"You ready to do this"

Emmit started wiping the steam off the bathroom mirror so he could check out his ripped pecs and abs. "I was ready to do this yesterday."

Omar gave him Myra's address and apartment number. "And Emmit, come alone."

Emmit stopped wiping down the mirror. "Sure, O, no problem. I'll see you in a bit." Emmit ended the call and walked out the bathroom. Shelly was lying on the bed on her stomach, in bra and panties, solving a Sudoku puzzle. Emmit smacked her on her butt.

"Get dressed. O just called with the address." He hit speed dial on his phone. "Get down here," Emmit said to Kay-Long, who was holed up in a motel room on the second floor.

Kay-Long tapped on Emmit's motel door ten minutes later. Shelly let him in. She was now wearing a black blouse with a pair of black stretch jeans. Emmit walked out of the bedroom holding a velvet gift bag by the drawstrings. The bag contained every penny he had to his name.

Shelly eyed him as she slid one bullet at a time into the barrel of her rubber grip, hammerless, .38 special. "Where's your piece?"

"Not bringing one," Emmit said nonchalantly.

She snapped the barrel shut and spun it. "Why?"

"Because I know Moon's fat ass is going to want to search me. And if he sees I'm carrying a gun, he's going to get all skittish. I can't afford to have him watching my every move."

"So, how's he going to feel when he searches me and finds that I'm carrying one?"

"I'm going in alone; we're switching to plan B."

"What?" Shelly exclaimed.

"Bad move, E," Kay-Long chimed in.

"Omar told me to come alone."

"I don't care what he told you," Shelly barked. "You're not walking in there by yourself."

"Shelly—"

"No, Emmit. It's too dangerous. Number one, you don't know how many people are in that apartment. Number two, you only have seventeen grand in that bag, the other twelve is monopoly money. What if that skittish motherfucker wants to count the money? And number three, for all we know, they could be setting you up to just take the cash and murder you."

Emmit walked up on her. "I got this." He looked at Kay-Long for his input.

"I say we stay with plan A. We've never done plan B."

"We can't always stick with plan A," Emmit said. "Things change, shit happens."

"Plan B is a shitty plan," Shelly said.

"It's an excellent plan," Emmit said with authority. "You ready to do this, Kay?"

Kay-Long opened his trench, exposing the butt of his shotgun. "Plan B is risky, but these fools ain't gonna see it coming until it came and we in the wind."

"That's what I want to hear," Emmit said pounding his fist against Kay-Long's. He then turned to Shelly. "I need you to be with me a hundred percent on this."

"I'm always a hundred percent with you."

"That's the Shelly I know and love." Emmit slid on his suit jacket and fastened one button. "Let's do this."

Emmit took the elevator while Shelly and Kay-Long took the stairs. He didn't approach Myra's apartment until he saw Shelly and Kay-Long tucked in the stairwell. He nodded at them. He could tell Shelly wasn't feeling this at all, but she was going to see it through to the end. Emmit knocked on the door.

Moon turned off the TV. Omar stepped out of the kitchen and looked through the peephole.

"I'm searching that motherfucker," Moon said.

Omar twisted his lips up at him. "Would you chill? We ain't trying to rub him the wrong way and have him wanting to find someone else to cop from."

"I'm not rubbing him. I'm patting him down."

Omar opened the door. "E, what up? You didn't have a hard time finding the place did you?"

"Nah, the cabbie knew exactly where it was," Emmit said, as he stepped in and bumped fists with Omar's. He then looked toward Moon. "What up, Moon?"

"You holding?" Moon asked, skipping the pleasantries.

Emmit smiled. "Nah, I don't need a gun amongst friends, right?"

"Well, being that we friends, you wouldn't mind if I pat you down right quick."

Emmit chuckled while looking at Omar. "Is he serious?"

"Don't sweat it," Omar said, trying to make it seem trivial. "He does this to everybody."

Emmit held his arms out and let Moon pat him down.

Moon tapped the flask of Don Q in Emmit's jacket and pulled it out.

Emmit shrugged. "I figured we'd solidify our arrangement with a toast."

Omar nodded and then snapped his fingers at Moon. "Go find us some glasses."

Moon looked down his nose at Emmit as he turned around and lumbered into the kitchen.

Omar put his arm around Emmit. "You know he can't stand you, right?"

"He never could, but that's okay. I'm not here for him to like me." Emmit handed the velvet gift bag to Omar. "Thirty grand, as agreed."

Omar weighed the bag in his hand and smiled. "I don't care what Moon says about you, you're alright with me."

Moon returned from the kitchen with a coffee cup, a beer mug, and a plastic tumbler. Omar furrowed his eyebrows "This bitch ain't got two of nothing," Moon said, placing the cups on the table.

"Bitch?" Emmit asked.

"Myra," Omar said, pointing to the bedroom. "This is her place."

Emmit nodded. "Then, maybe we should invite her out here and offer her a shot of this Don Q."

"The only shot she's interested in is the one going into her arm," Moon snorted.

Emmit smiled. "Okay, allow me." He opened the flask of Don Q and poured them each a shot, then held his glass up. "To a fruitful future."

Omar picked up the coffee cup, Moon the mug. They both watched Emmit throw back his shot before each of them drank theirs. Emmit poured each of them two more shots.

"Okay," Emmit said after polishing off his last shot. "You got the money, so where's the squares?"

Omar nodded to Moon. Moon disappeared into the kitchen and came back with the two squares of heroin and placed them in front of Emmit and began opening one. Emmit stopped him.

"That's not necessary, I trust you."

Moon shrugged and placed the two bricks of heroin into a shopping bag.

Omar tossed Moon the velvet gift bag. Moon opened it and began dumping the money onto the table. Emmit almost bit his tongue.

"Yo, what the fuck are you doing?" Omar said.

"I'm counting the money."

"Man… I gave you the bag to put away, not to count the money. E isn't going to come up in here, by himself, unarmed, and try to stiff us."

Emmit smiled and poured himself another shot. If Omar was paying attention, he would've noticed the beads of sweat on Emmit's forehead.

Moon stuffed the few stacks that fell onto the table back into the bag and disappeared back into the kitchen.

Emmit started shaking his leg. "Woo, wee, that Don is running through me. I have to take a serious leak. Let me use the bathroom and then I'm out of here."

"Straight in the back," Omar said, pointing.

"Good looking," Emmit said, heading to the back.

Myra stood by her bedroom door the whole time. She held her breath as Emmit walked past. She heard the bathroom door open and then shut. "Just hurry the fuck up and get out of my house," she whispered.

Emmit pulled out his cell phone and texted Shelly.

Omar and Moon, in living room, dope fiend bitch in back bedroom. On my way out.

Emmit closed his phone. He flushed the toilet and then washed his hands. "Okay," he whispered to himself. "Let's do this."

Myra heard the bathroom door open and shut. She cracked her door and caught a glimpse of Emmit's profile as he walked by. Her heart was beating between her ears. Something wasn't right. She heard the toilet flush, she heard the faucet run, but what she didn't hear was Emmit piss. The apartment walls were so thin that even if he pissed against the side of the bowl, she would've heard it. *Please don't let this fool try nothing stupid.*

When Emmit returned to the living room, Moon was holding the shopping bag in his hand.

"I would love to catch up on old times," Omar said, "but Moon and I have some other business to tend to. Perhaps another time." Moon shoved the bag against Emmit's chest.

"Yeah," Emmit said. "There will be plenty of time for us to catch up."

Moon headed to the door, Emmit was three steps behind him.

Shelly and Kay-long stood on either side of the door with their backs flushed to the wall. Both heard the lock being disengaged and nodded to each other. Moon opened the door. He saw the butt of Kay-long's shotgun too late. Kay-long cracked him on the jaw, knocking him out cold. Emmit stomped on Moon's head a couple times to make sure he was unconscious. Kay-long kept moving. He ran up on Omar and pointed his shotgun at his chest.

"Yo, yo, what the fuck? This is how you gonna do me, E?"

Emmit ignored him for the moment. "Bedroom on the right," he said to Shelly, telling her where Myra was. Shelly handed him a gun and headed toward the bedroom.

"Shit, shit, shit, I fucking knew it." Myra's hands were balled so tight her nails were digging into the flesh of her palms. She heard Shelly trying to tiptoe toward her room, but she may as well have been wearing bells. In battle-mode Myra could hear an ant pissing on cotton during rush hour. Myra sat on her bed and pretended to be in a dope-induced nod. It was obvious that this crew wasn't intent on killing anybody, at least not yet.

Shelly busted into the room and pointed her gun at Myra. "Hey." Myra didn't flinch. "Hey, bitch, get up."

Myra slowly looked up and then let her head drop.

Shelly huffed. "Just my luck." She grabbed Myra by the front of her sweat hood and pulled her to her feet. "Come on, let's go."

Myra got to her feet and slurred, "Can you talk to Omar and see if he'll give me another bag on credit?"

"You can talk to him yourself. Move." Shelly pushed her out of the bedroom and into the living room.

Myra took in the scene. Moon was flat on his back, knocked out. Omar was standing against the wall with a beefy man in a trench coat pointing a sawed-off shotgun at him. A man of Asian descent walked out of the kitchen, holding a velvet bag. He looked at Myra and deemed her to be harmless.

Three, Myra thought. They bust in and round everybody up in the living room. She smiled. No matter how much she tried to escape her past, it always came back to haunt her.

"Something funny?" Shelly asked Myra.

"Talk to Omar," Myra pretended to slur. "See if he'll let me—" Shelly shoved her against the wall.

"Easy," Emmit said. "She's high out her mind."

"Then she shouldn't feel anything when I put two in her head."

"Easy," Emmit said.

"All the money you making, and you have to pinch me for a couple squares?" Omar said to Emmit.

"A couple squares here, a couple squares there, and before you know it, I'm sitting on enough bricks to build a fortune. Now that I have what I came for, you need to give me a reason why I should let you live."

"C'mon, E," Omar said with a jittery voice. "Like you said, you got what you came for."

"Yeah, I got what I came for, but I'm gonna need a little more persuasion. I'm sure you have a little something stashed, right here."

"There's nothing here, E. I would never keep anything in a dope fiend's house."

"On the contrary, I think you would." Emmit cocked the hammer on his gun. "Just tell me where the stash is and you'll live to make back whatever I take from you."

"I'm telling you, E, there's nothing here."

"I don't believe you." Emmit turned his gun on Moon and shot him in the head. Omar started to scream, but closed his mouth when Kay-long put the shotgun to his head.

"She's next," Emmit said, pointing to Myra.

"In the ceiling," Myra blurted out.

Emmit looked at her.

"The ceiling," Myra said again pointing up to a single spot in the drop ceiling.

Emmit looked at Omar.

"She's crazy, E," Omar said. "Ain't shit in that ceiling."

"Oh really?" Emmit said, trying to read Omar's facial expression. He turned to Myra and pointed to the ceiling with his gun. "It's your house, so do us the honors and go get it."

Myra didn't move.

"Move!" Shelly shoved her.

Myra stumbled and fell.

Emmit shook his head as he looked Myra in the eye. "Get up and get me what I want or you're going to be lying next to Moon over there."

Myra got to her feet and shuffled toward Emmit to get to the spot in the ceiling she had pointed to. The look of fear in Myra's eyes made him lower his defenses. It also made Shelly lower her gun, but she made sure she stayed three steps behind Myra. Myra counted how many steps she had before she would be near Emmit. Five, four, three, two…

CHAPTER 3

*I*n one fluid motion, Myra grabbed the flask of Don Q off the table by its neck and swung it at Emmit's face. Her movement was too quick and too accurate for Emmit, Shelly, or Kay-Long to do anything but stare in disbelief as Myra broke the bottle on Emmit's face. He dropped the money, the dope, and yelled as he reared back and grabbed the bridge of his nose.

Myra didn't break stride, she used the momentum of the swing to keep turning. Shelly raised her gun, Myra grabbed her by the wrist and stabbed her in the throat with the jagged end of the bottle. Shelly took in a sharp breath of air and stared at Myra in disbelief. The gun slipped from her hand. Myra caught it and let go of Shelly.

Kay-Long pulled the trigger, blowing Omar's head off his shoulders. It would take Kay-Long two seconds to pump another shell into the chamber and point the shotgun at Myra. She only needed one. She trained the .38 on Kay-Long and fired twice. Both bullets made identical holes in his forehead. Emmit finally wiped the gushing blood out of his eyes and charged Myra. She stopped him with two shots to the chest.

Four seconds Myra estimated; three bodies in four seconds. She looked at the carnage and punched the wall. "Shit, shit, shit." She raced to her bedroom and grabbed a tote bag from out the closet and ran back into the living room. Two minutes, Myra guessed. Two minutes to get out before the police arrived. She dug through the corpses for anything that the police could use to identify them.

She stuffed their wallets, cell phones, and car keys in her tote bag. Without identification, it would take the police a couple days to identify all of the bodies. She stuffed Omar's car keys in her front pocket and froze. The velvet bag and brown shopping bag containing the two bricks of dope was staring her in the face. She scooped them up under her arm and dashed out of the apartment and down the stairwell.

The two officers dispatched to investigate possible gunshots walked into the lobby of Myra's apartment building.

"What floor was it?" Officer Webster asked his partner. Officer Webster was a five-nine, beefy, angry black man.

"Dispatch said it was the fifth floor," Webster's partner, Officer Rose said. Officer Rose was a five-five, buck twenty, with all his gear on, baby-faced rookie.

"This elevator better be working, 'cause I'm not trying to climb all them stairs; I'm going on twelve hours without sleep," Webster said, as he pressed the elevator call button.

Myra cleared the last group of steps and busted out of the stairwell. She skidded to a halt when she spotted the officers and they spotted her.

Shit, Myra said to herself as she rushed toward them crying. "There's people shooting upstairs."

Officer Rose, the rookie, put his hand on the butt of his gun.

Webster stuck his hand out to stop Myra. "Ma'am, I'm going to need you to remain calm."

Myra looked behind her as she steadily rushed toward them. "Three men, upstairs."

"Ma'am—" Webster started to say.

"Freeze!" Rose said, as he started to draw his gun. Myra stopped in her tracks, eyes wide, five feet away.

Webster turned to Rose. "What are you doing? Put your gun—"

Myra leaped forward. Rose's eyes grew wide like saucers. Myra grabbed his wrist, while simultaneously folding Webster in half with a front thrust kick to his groin. While still holding Officer Rose's wrist, Myra pivoted under the rookie's arm and judo flipped him to the ground. She kicked him in the face and wrenched his gun from him and thumbed off the safety.

Myra quickly looked around. In the takedown, she dropped the tote bag and the dope. The tote bag had slid near the building's entrance, while the bag of dope lay near officer Webster, who was still struggling to suck air into his lungs. Myra went for the shopping bag, Webster reached for his gun. Myra had a choice. Shoot a cop and grab the dope or take off while she still had a chance. She thought about how long two kilos of dope would keep her high and made up her mind. She shot Webster in the chest.

Myra reached for the bag of dope and a shot rang out. Officer Rose had gotten to his backup gun housed in his ankle holster. Myra dove to the ground and returned fire, hitting Rose with two bullets to the chest. He slumped against the wall, wincing in pain. Rose and Webster's bulletproof vests stopped the bullets from penetrating, but they didn't stop their impact. Rose had two broken ribs, Webster one.

Myra's shoulder was on fire. She couldn't tell the extent of the damage, not with her adrenaline running on high, so she forgot about the kilos of dope. She snatched up the tote bag on her way out and searched for Omar's car. It was nowhere in sight. Her head jerked up when she heard police sirens. She looked toward the police car and then back into the building. What was the chance of them leaving the keys in the ignition? A very good one. Myra hopped in and peeled off.

Myra listened to the police radio while she tried to put as much distance between her and the crime scene. She played the scene over and over in her head. Emmit had left her no choice. The way he nonchalantly shot Moon told her that he had the same thing planned for her and Omar. She parked down the block from a cabstand and pulled her arm out of her sweat hood. The rookie's bullet had grazed her shoulder. Her T-shirt had soaked up most of the blood so she didn't have to worry about people noticing blood on her hoodie. She abandoned the police car and pulled one of the cell phones out of her tote bag and made a call.

"Peace be upon you," Myra said in Arabic when the person on the other end of the line picked up.

"And peace be upon you," the woman responded wearily.

"I need a car and a place to stay, and I need them in that order," Myra snapped off in fluent Arabic.

"Is everything okay?"

"*Our* plans haven't been compromised, but I got myself into a little jam; nothing I can't get myself out of." The woman didn't respond. "Are you still there?"

"Do you still have the suitcases?" the woman finally responded.

"Not with me, but—"

The woman started cursing in Arabic.

"Hey," Myra yelled. "They're secure. Everything's still a go."

"Everything's not a go unless I say so."

Myra sucked her teeth. "I need that car and place."

"Where are you?"

"Manhattan, East side."

"There's a parking garage on 132nd between 7th avenue and Lenox."

"I know it," Myra said hurriedly.

"The man in the booth will be expecting you."

"And the place to stay?" Myra reminded her.

"Can't help you with that."

"What do you mean you can't—"

The woman hung up.

Myra gripped the phone, tempted to throw it to the ground, but she dismantled it instead and discarded the pieces one by one as she headed to the cabstand.

Myra had the cab drop her off a block away from the parking garage and walked the rest of the way. The man in the booth closed his newspaper when he saw her approaching.

"You're expecting me," Myra said in Arabic when she got to the booth. The man nodded and handed her a matchbook and a keyless remote. She snatched them from him and headed up the ramp. The man had scribbled the location of the car on the inside flap of the matchbook. It didn't take Myra long to find the car. It was a brown Malibu.

Forty-five minutes later, Myra pulled up to Jamie Towers. Omar owned a co-op in the first building. The only ones who knew about this apartment were Omar, Moon, and Myra. She found out about it when she was bored one night and decided to follow Omar to his home away from home. Myra collapsed on the couch and closed her eyes. She could tell from the stale air trapped inside the unit that Omar hadn't been here in a while. Myra got off the couch and found the bathroom and the first aid kit. She removed her hoodie and T-shirt and inspected the wound a little closer than she did before. She cleaned the scratch with peroxide and slapped a large Band-Aid on it. The fridge was packed with bottled water and microwavable food. Myra nodded. After she ate, she was going to sleep like a hibernating bear.

Dr. Randal had her coat and purse in one hand and her keys in the other as she exited her office. She sorted through the keys with her thumb and forefinger until she came across the one to her office. Everyone on her floor left an hour ago, which was why she looked over her shoulder when she heard hard-bottom shoes approaching her from behind. The man approaching her was tall, his skin the color of oak. His blue suit was impressively pressed, his overcoat conformed to his lean frame perfectly. His haircut and clean-shave made him look like he just stood up from the barber's chair. He smiled and extended his hand toward Dr. Randal.

"Dr. Randal, forgive me for showing up unannounced."

Laura shook his hand. He had a firm grip. "I was just on my way out."

The man reached in his coat and pulled out his ID. "Sergeant Andrew Cleary, U.S. Army."

"Okay," Laura said, studying his ID.

"I just need a few moments of your time."

"If you can come back tomorrow—"

"Time's not on my side; I really need to speak with you regarding one of your clients."

"Sergeant Cleary—"

"Call me Andrew."

"Andrew, I'm sorry, but I can't discuss any of—"

"Listen, Doc..." Andrew's tone sent a chill down Laura's spine. "Officially I'm not here."

"Then, I suggest you come back tomorrow, officially. Now, if you'll excuse me."

"Myra Taft is wanted for multiple murders and attempt murder on two police officers."

Laura's mouth dropped open.

"The police are labeling it as a drug-buy gone bad. Five people were murdered in Myra's apartment."

"Five?"

"Five. And as she was fleeing the scene, she shot two officers who confronted her in the lobby of her apartment building. Luckily they were both wearing vests."

"My God."

"She's on the run and I need to locate her before the police do and hopefully before you receive an 'official' visit from the Army."

Laura was too stunned to say anything.

"Doc, if the shit wasn't about to hit the fan, I wouldn't be here."

Laura regained her composure. "I don't know how I can be of any help without breaking confidentiality."

Sergeant Cleary smiled, but Laura could tell it was a smile to mask his frustration with her. She wanted to help Myra in any way she could, but she couldn't just give up her clients's information to anyone who came around asking.

Sergeant Cleary withdrew one of his personal business cards and handed it to her. "If she attempts to contact you, it's imperative that you call me immediately."

"And if I don't?" Laura asked.

"Excuse me?"

"What if I don't want to call? What if I prefer to wait for the 'official' visit from the Army?" Laura stiffened when she saw the flash of anger cross Sergeant Cleary's face before he had a chance to mask it with his smile. He looked her in the eyes.

"I know you'll do what's best for Myra." He bowed slightly and headed back toward the elevators.

Myra sat in Omar's apartment most of the night watching the news and weighing her options. The news-breaking story was on all the major TV networks. She turned up the TV to hear the latest from a reporter who was standing in front of her building.

"Police are speculating that this was a drug buy gone bad. Five are dead, but haven't yet been identified. The sixth person escaped from the apartment and on her way out got into a shootout with the first officers to arrive on the scene. The woman, who police have identified as Myra Taft shot the two officers and made a speedy getaway in their police cruiser." A sketch that both Webster and Rose helped compose came onto the screen. "Anyone coming into contact with this woman is being asked not to approach her. She's considered armed and extremely dangerous."

"I'll be on America's Most Wanted by the end of the week," Myra said with a sigh. Right now, a bundle of dope was on Myra's Most Wanted. Her stomach had been in knots since yesterday. She thought about the seventeen thousand she counted in the velvet bag, after she separated it from the counterfeit money, and then pictured herself in high-def snorting a bundle up each nostril. "Fuck this, I'm out."

Myra sat in the Malibu right outside Castle Hill projects, located right across from Jamie Towers. The streets of Castle Hill weren't that bad in the daytime, but come night, the streets were the last place you'd want to be. And you better stay far away from your windows; stray bullets had a funny way of finding their way through project windows.

Myra had been watching a kid hanging out by the bus stop doing hand-to-hand transactions. She couldn't tell what he was selling, but she was sure that if it wasn't dope, he could direct her to someone who was. She pulled her hoodie over her head and got out the car.

She walked past him and into the bodega where she bought a pack of Newports and a lighter. She exited the store and stood by the bus stop and lit a cigarette.

"What's good?" Myra asked, not bothering to look the kid in the eye.

"What's good with you?" the kid responded, never taking his eyes off her.

"I'm looking to get right."

The kid looked at the Malibu he saw her get out of and then looked back at her. "And what's right for you, ma?"

Myra sniffled. "A bundle."

The kid arched an eyebrow. "I don't know what you're talking about."

Myra took a long pull off her cigarette and then stamped it out under her foot. She pulled up the left sleeve of her hoodie and held her arm out to him. "You know what I'm talking about now?"

The kid stared at the needle marks and nodded. She definitely wasn't Five-O. He pulled out his cell and dialed a number. "Got one for you. A bundle, you heard?" He ended the call. "You want haze to go with that, ma?" He figured he'd try and sell her the last two bags of weed he had.

"The bundle is good enough."

A few minutes later, another kid turned the corner. He pushed the rest of his burger into his mouth and wiped his hands on his pants. He gave his man a pound and looked at

Myra. She didn't bother pulling down her sleeve. He saw the needle tracks on her arm and nodded while pulling out the bundle. Myra and the kid made the swap, hand-over-fist.

"You want some company to go with that?" the new kid asked, as he ogled her.

"I have all the company I need right here," Myra said, tapping the bundle she just slid into her hoodie. She quickly crossed the street to the Malibu and pulled off.

Myra was back in the apartment, drooling with anticipation. She broke open a bag and set up four lines to snort. She knocked them off without batting an eye. She sat back and closed her eyes. A thought crossed her mind. She tapped her back pocket, remembering that she still had Dr. Randal's card. She pulled it out and read off Laura's home number before pulling out one of the cell phones in her tote bag.

Laura cracked an eyelid when she heard her phone ringing. No one called her this late at night. She jumped up and answered it. Last time she had gotten a call this late, it was a family member telling her that her uncle had died. "Hello," she answered while wiping the sleep out her eyes.

"What's up Doc?" Myra started laughing. "I always wanted to say that. You get it? Bugs Bunny?"

Laura sat up, fully alert. "Myra, where are you. You sound out of it."

"I've been nodding off and on." Myra laughed at her private joke.

"I saw you on the news today, Myra."

"They're lying, Doc. Don't believe a word of what they're saying."

"They said five people were murdered in your apartment in a drug deal gone wrong, and that you shot two police officers. None of that is true?"

"Actually, that's pretty accurate, only I'm not the bad guy in all this. I fucked up, Doc. I allowed Omar to do a deal in my apartment. I didn't know that the buyer was going to try and rob him. I just want you to know that I didn't want to kill anyone. They were going to kill me."

"Jesus, Myra."

"I don't know what to do, Doc."

"You're going to have to turn yourself in."

"That's not going to happen. Five homicides, attempt murder on police, the judge will probably give me life without parole and then the death penalty." Myra chuckled. "I'm a dead man walking."

"Don't say that."

"It's true. There's nothing anyone can do for me."

"There might be someone. A friend of yours visited me this evening."

"I don't have any friends."

"He said he was from the Army. His name's Sergeant Cleary."

"Describe him."

"Uh… brown-skinned, tall…"

"Gray eyes?"

"I think so."

"I don't need you to think, Doc, I need you to know. Gray or not?"

"Yes, he had gray eyes."

Myra felt like an icy fist had just closed over her heart.

"Is he a friend or not?" Laura asked.

"Like I said, Doc, I don't have any friends. I have to go."

"Wait, what about the police?"

"Right now, the police are the least of my worries. Nice knowing you, Doc. I wish you the best, take care."

"Myra wait!" Myra ended the call. Laura checked her caller ID and called the number back. Myra didn't answer. Laura thought about calling Sergeant Cleary, but remembered Myra's words; *she didn't have any friends.*

Laura sat behind her desk the following afternoon, leafing through Myra's file. It was thick, that was to be expected for someone who was in the Army for twelve years, but there was something about Myra's file that didn't seem right.

"Dr. Randal." Laura's secretary poked her head in Laura's office. "Sorry to bother you. Major Jennings is here to see you. He says it's important."

Laura fumbled with Myra's folder as she tried to close it and slide it in her drawer at the same time. "Show him in."

Major Jennings walked in with his coat and hat in hand. With his gray hair and narrow face wrapped in wrinkles, he looked every bit of sixty, with a lot of those years being hard.

"Dr. Randal." He shook her hand and sat down.

"Major, it's nice to see you."

"The pleasure's always mine."

Laura sighed. "I only wish seeing you wasn't under these circumstances."

"So you've heard?"

"Myra's been all over the news for the past two days. The police are saying it was a drug deal gone bad. I can't believe that. Myra's not a drug dealer, and she sure as hell isn't a drug user. There has to be some other explanation."

Major Jennings remained silent for a minute. "Myra's been attending her sessions with you, right?"

"Of course."

"Did she give you any indication that she was dealing or using drugs?"

"Of course not; I would've contacted you immediately. I definitely didn't see this coming."

Major Jennings reached into his pocket. "Forgive me, but I have to go through the formalities with you." He pulled out a document and handed it to her.

Laura stared at the copy of the confidential agreement she signed when she agreed to take on Myra as a client. "I don't understand. Why are you showing me—" She understood when she saw the highlighted paragraph near the bottom. It stipulated that under no circumstance was she to discuss her findings or observations regarding Specialist Myra Taft to anyone without an Army representative present. A breach of confidentiality on her part could be punishable with imprisonment.

Major Jennings spoke, "The police found a dresser drawer full of antidepressants that you prescribed for her. My guess is detectives will be stopping by to question you."

"I imagine they will."

"And threaten you as they may, you don't have to answer any questions. You wave this in their faces and they have to back off. And just so you know, the Army is doing their own separate investigation so I'm going to need the file on Myra that I supplied you with, as well as your personal notes you have on her."

"Excuse me?"

"Dr. Randal—"

Laura stood up. "I have an obligation to my client."

"She's no longer your client."

Laura opened her drawer and slid him the file he gave her on Myra. "The folder is Army property, my notes on Myra is mine. And I'm not handing those over; not without Myra's consent or some kind of court order."

Major Jennings got to his feet. "Dr. Randal don't do this. You can't win against the U.S. Army."

Laura could see the fire behind his eyes. She could tell he wasn't used to being told no. "I'm sorry, Major, but just like the Army has its rules and regulations, I have mine. I'm sure you can understand that."

Major Jennings cracked a smile. "I understand. If Myra tries to contact you—"

"I'll give you a call."

Major Jennings picked up the folder and left.

Laura crossed her arms. Every muscle in her shoulders was tensed. Major Jennings was one of the Army's best psychologists. Surely he could have taken Myra on as a client, especially when it came to Post Traumatic Stress Disorder. He was more of an expert in that field than she ever would be. *Guess that was the 'official' visit* Laura thought. She thought of the conversation between her and Sergeant Cleary—The shit had definitely hit the fan.

CHAPTER 4

Dr. Randal locked her office door and headed to the elevator. It had been another long day. And as usual, she was the last one to leave the 7th floor. But she couldn't say the day wasn't interesting. Major Jennings was right. Two detectives paid her a visit and grilled her like she was a suspect. They even went as far as insinuating that maybe she was writing scripts for Myra to fill so that she could pass the pills off to the dealers who would peddle the pills on the streets. Dr. Randal came close to getting arrested for assault by the way she was yelling in their faces. The elevator opened up into the garage. She stepped out and headed to her car. Right now, all she wanted to do was go home, relax, and listen to her...

"Shit." She turned around and headed back to the elevator. She left her Rihanna CD in her office. The elevator door swooshed open onto the 7th floor. Laura headed to her office. She stopped short when she saw her office door ajar. She was about to panic but then she saw the janitor's cleaning cart. She walked into her office.

The janitor looked up. The surprised look on his face told Laura that he was up to no good. Laura understood the reason for his facial expression when she saw her file drawers open and her computer on. She quickly lost interest in what the janitor was doing when she noticed the black gloves on the his hands.

Her survival instincts kicked in. She took off, making sure to pull the cleaning cart in front of the door. She heard when the janitor crashed into the cleaning cart as he took off after her. She blew past the elevator and banged open the staircase door with her shoulder. She chanced a look over her shoulder and screamed. The janitor was almost on her. She ran down the steps as fast as her heels would allow her, screaming for help all the while. Someone had to be in the building.

She grunted as a hand shoved her from behind. She lost her balance and tumbled down a flight of stairs. She landed on her side with her back against the wall. She moaned as her head spun and as pain rippled through her body. Gloved hands wrapped themselves around her neck and started squeezing. It took Laura a couple of seconds to realize she couldn't breathe.

No, she thought. She was too disorientated to say it out loud. She pounded at the hands with her fists as she fought for air. She squirmed and twisted, but he wouldn't let go. All the moving she did put a little space between them. Laura brought her knee up with the last little bit of strength she had left. She kneed the janitor in the groin. He released his grip and grabbed his crotch.

Laura wobbled to her feet and stumbled through the 5th floor stairwell door. She hobbled to the elevator and kept hitting the call button until she heard the elevator making its way up. Her head whipped toward the stairwell when she heard the door bang open. The Janitor started running toward her with a knife in his hand. Laura screamed and banged on the elevator door. She backed away from the elevator as the janitor came at her.

"Please," she begged. She fell backward on her butt. The janitor looked around to make sure there were no witnesses, and then focused back on Laura. She thought of begging for her life, but the look on the janitor's face told her she should use the little time she had left to pray.

The elevator chimed and the doors opened. "Hey!"

The janitor turned around.

Sergeant Cleary saw the knife in the janitor's hand and Laura on the floor. The janitor rushed toward him. He slashed and jabbed at Cleary who fluidly evaded the knife's razor edge. The janitor got four swings off before Sergeant Cleary went from defense to offense. On the janitor's fifth swing, Cleary stepped in, grabbing the janitor's wrist while slipping under the janitor's armpit. He judo flipped him. The janitor scrambled to his feet and backed into the elevator just as it was closing. Sergeant Cleary tried sticking his hand between the doors but he was too late. He pounded the door with his fist. He looked at the stairwell and then looked at Laura trembling on the floor. He approached her and kneeled beside her.

"Are you okay?"

She nodded and then fainted.

Laura didn't start regaining her bearings until Cleary laid her down on the couch in her office. She watched him through blurry eyes as he stood behind her desk looking at the computer screen.

"You can't do that." Laura's voice was weak.

"You don't have to worry about me prying; your computer's hard drive has been wiped clean."

Laura sighed and slowly sat up. Sergeant Cleary walked from around the desk and leaned on it. "Are you going to be okay?"

"No. Someone broke into my office, erased all my files, and then tried to kill me." Her bottom lip started to quiver as the true weight of what transpired sunk in. "I have to call the police." She started to get up. Her legs wobbled. Sergeant Cleary rushed over to her and grabbed her by the arms.

"Just rest for a moment." He guided her back down onto the couch and sat beside her.

"I can't believe Major Jennings would do something like this," Laura said.

"Jennings?" Cleary said surprised.

"He paid me an 'official' visit this afternoon. He wanted the file he gave me on Myra and my notes."

"And you didn't give them to him."

"I gave him the file, but I didn't give him my notes. Which is why he sent that... whoever the hell he was to steal them."

"You're talking about a highly decorated Major in the United States Army. He doesn't have to resort to burglary to get files, and he would never sanction murder."

"I walked in on the guy. I got a good look at his face, he probably thought he had no choice."

Cleary shook his head. "You're wrong about the Major."

"Am I? He comes to my office this afternoon wanting my personal notes on Myra, and when I refuse, a man breaks into my office. That's a hell of a coincidence."

"Everything isn't always as it seems, Doc."

"Exactly." Laura was looking at him, but her mind was someplace else. She realized what was wrong with Myra's folder.

"Are you okay, Doc?"

"As many times as I read Myra's folder, I can't believe I missed it."

"Missed what?" Cleary asked.

"Myra's folder was thick as a telephone book, yet there was nothing in it about her combat history."

"Myra was a communications specialist, she wasn't a combat soldier."

Laura shook her head. "No, in our last session, she said she *fought* for her country. When I talked to her about pain, she became animated and used the word *betrayal*. I'm not an expert in warfare, but I know a soldier restricted to communications wouldn't use words like fought and betrayal."

"I think you're losing it, Doc."

"I think I'm finding it. Everything isn't as it seems. That's what you said. What if everyone isn't who they seem?"

"Doc?"

"I spoke with Myra last night. She knew who you were, but she made it clear that you weren't a friend."

Sergeant Cleary grabbed her by her shoulders. "You spoke to her? Why didn't you call me?"

"You're hurting me."

Sergeant Cleary let her go. "I'm sorry, I didn't mean to, I just..." Cleary held his head back as if he was trying to stop a nosebleed. What he was trying to stop was the tears. Laura stared at him, not knowing how to react or what to say. Cleary dropped his head and looked at her for a moment, then he pulled out his wallet and handed her a photo.

Laura stared at the photo, wide-eyed. Cleary stood in back of Myra with his arms around her waist. Myra had her hands on top of his. Laura focused on the ring.

"I love my wife," Cleary started. "but when she came back from Iraq, she wasn't the same. Those bastards... the things they did to her..." Cleary was wringing his hands. "When she came back, she was just a shell. I couldn't deal with that, so I left."

"Left?"

"I requested a transfer and I filed for a divorce."

"How could you just leave your wife?"

"Don't, Doc, don't judge me."

"I'm not—"

"Yes, you are. If I loved her like I said, how could I just leave her? I'll tell you how; I was a coward. I could fight on the frontlines for my country, but I couldn't even help my wife with the battle she was fighting within. She was broken and I didn't know how to help her put the pieces back together. So, I left. I couldn't bring myself to finalize the divorce. I thought that maybe one day..."

"Laura gripped his hand. "I'm so sorry."

"I'm the one who should be sorry. I should've been totally honest with you, but I had to know if I could trust you."

Laura nodded. "You can trust me. So Myra wasn't in communications, was she?"

Cleary contemplated on whether or not he should answer her question. "Myra started out in communications, but her wits and strong will made her the perfect candidate for the Army's M.O.P. unit. Military Offense Program."

Laura's belly jumped. She wanted to stop him, but her curiosity wouldn't allow her.

"Myra was the best at what she did."

"And what was that?"

"Infiltration. She had a knack for infiltrating certain groups."

"Like the terrorist groups in Iraq?" Laura asked.

Cleary chuckled. "And in Afghanistan, and in Pakistan, and in Yemen, and the list goes on."

"How did she—"

Cleary held his hand up. "I already told you too much."

"I'm sorry, I didn't mean to press."

Cleary squeezed her hand. "I don't care what my wife told you, she's not stable. I don't know what happened in that apartment, and I don't know why she shot those officers, but I do know one thing. She's not going to allow the police to arrest her. If I can locate her and talk her in, the Army will protect her."

"Protect her how?" Laura asked.

"Once she's in army custody, we can sling around enough red tape to choke out the media frenzy. From there, our psychologists can prove to a jury that Myra wasn't in her right state of mind."

"Post-Traumatic Stress Disorder," Laura said, seeing where Cleary was going with it.

"And whatever else our psychologists can diagnose her with."

"You shouldn't be telling me this," Laura said.

"I'm telling you because I need your help in finding her."

Laura looked into his eyes and saw nothing but love and concern. She looked back to the photo of Myra and smiled. "So, this is what she looked like with hair."

"Yeah, that picture was taken before she went G.I. Jane on us."

Laura handed him back the photo. "I don't know how I can help you. She called me last night, told me the facts about what happened in her apartment were true, but she did what she did because they were going to kill her."

"Who was going to kill her?"

"The people who were there to purchase the drugs. They may have come there with the intent of taking the drugs and killing everyone, I guess."

"She didn't tell you where she was?"

"No, but now that I think about it…"

"Think about what?"

"I might be wrong, but she sounded like she was drunk or high. The way her words were slurring, and the way she was making jokes."

"High?" Cleary repeated."

"I know it sounds crazy, but—"

"No, it doesn't. Some people use drugs when coping with reality becomes too hard; and with what she's been through, getting high would be the perfect way of not having to deal with what happened to her."

"I can't believe I didn't see the signs," Laura said.

"Myra's good at concealing things; so don't be too hard on yourself. Did she say anything else?"

"After I told her about you, she became agitated. She wished me the best and told me to take care."

Cleary sighed. "That doesn't sound good."

"I know, that's why I tried calling her back, but she wouldn't answer."

Cleary eyes widened. "You have the number she actually called you from?"

"Yes, it's still in my cell phone."

Cleary started pulling his cell phone out as he stood up. "I need that number, Doc."

Laura picked her bag off the floor and pulled out her cell phone and scrolled down the recent calls. "Here's it is." She handed him her phone.

Cleary dialed a number on his phone. "Got a number," he said when the other party picked up. "(917) 236-5656." Cleary closed his eyes as he waited. He opened his eyes and looked right at Laura when the person on the other end gave him a name. "Did Myra ever mention the name Omar Sanders?"

"Omar... yes, Myra called the drug dealer Omar."

Cleary spoke to the other person on the line. "Call me immediately when you find that phone."

"What do you mean by find that phone?" Laura asked.

"A person with the right software can access the GPS of any person's phone."

"Are you serious?"

Cleary held out his hand to her. "I'll walk you to your car." Laura didn't move. "What's wrong?"

"Do you think my life is in danger? That guy got away. What if he knows where I live?"

"Do you have anyone you can stay with for the time being? A friend, a boyfriend, girlfriend?"

Laura shook her head. "I've been so focused on my work... I haven't had the time to keep in touch with friends and family. And to just show up at their doorstep now..."

Cleary's phone rang. "Yes... okay... I'll check it out." He ended the call.

"Any luck?" Laura asked.

"The phone's last GPS location was at Jamie Towers. Omar Sanders has an apartment there in his name."

"I'll go with you?"

"I can't risk putting you in harm's way, Doc."

"I'm already in danger; someone tried to kill me, remember?"

"Doc—"

"Can you think of a safer place for me to be right now?"

Cleary closed his eyes and rubbed the bridge of his nose. "Let's go, before I change my mind."

CHAPTER 5

*M*yra opened and closed her eyes. "Shit." She wiped the drool from her chin and looked around the apartment. She counted five empty bags on the table. The clock on the DVD said 5:45pm. Myra groaned as she stood up from the couch and stretched her arms over her head. She almost choked on the funk shooting from her armpits. If her memory served her right, she hadn't taken a shower in three days.

Omar's bathroom was modern, complete with an assortment of soaps and lotions. She stripped, grabbed a new bar of soap and stepped into the shower. The hot water felt good beating against her skin. Three minutes later, she was rinsing off and grabbing a towel off the rack. Myra never allowed herself to ever remain naked for too long. If she had to go out fighting, she didn't want to have to do it in the buff.

She wrapped herself in a towel and entered the bedroom. Omar's first closet had nothing but tracksuits and sneakers. The pants, skirts, and blouses in the second closet would have been okay if they weren't two sizes smaller than what Myra was used to wearing. She couldn't take the chance of putting her clothes back on. The cops she shot probably gave a description of what she was wearing.

"Fuck it," she mumbled. She needed to cop another bundle and stay moving. She wiggled into a pair of black stretch pants and a black blouse. She then grabbed a knit hat, a bandana, and a pair of shades and headed back into the living room where she stuffed her old clothes into her tote bag. She grabbed Omar's cell phone off the table along with her tote bag and left the apartment. She dismantled Omar's phone and dropped it in the incinerator on her way to the elevator.

Cleary just turned off the highway when his phone vibrated. "Yes."

Laura could tell by the way he gripped the steering wheel that something was wrong.

"Okay, I'm a half hour away." He ended the call.

"What's wrong?" Laura asked.

"The GPS on Omar's phone fizzled out."

"What does that mean?"

"Don't know," he said, but the look on his face and the needle on the speedometer jumping to seventy told Laura that whatever happened wasn't good.

Myra was back in Castle Hill projects, parked across the street from the same corner store. The kid selling weed was standing at the same bus stop talking on his cell. She got out and locked eyes with him as she walked past him and headed into the store. She exited the bodega, peeling the seal off the pack of Newports she just purchased. The kid folded his phone shut when she stood beside him.

"What's good, ma?" he asked, as he eyed her shapely hips.

"I need to holler at your man."

"Same as last time?" the kid asked.

Myra took a pull off the cigarette and then nodded.

The kid made the call. "It's me… shortie from the other night needs you to come through… yeah that's the one with the juicy lips.

Myra blew out a cloud of smoke and looked at the kid. He winked at her and closed his phone.

"He's on his way."

Dope boy rounded the corner, trying to look laid back, but Myra could see him trying to catch his breath. His eyes dropped to the tight pants and then lingered on the clingy blouse. He looked her in the eyes with a newfound respect. She wasn't just a dope fiend. She was a dope fiend with a banging body.

"Damn, ma," Dope boy said, licking his lips. "You must be coming from work, with the way you're all dressed up."

Myra pulled out two crisp one hundred dollar bills. "I'm in a rush."

Dope boy pulled the bundle from his pocket. They made the swap. He held onto her hand. "Looks like you can use some company."

Myra pulled her hand away. She sized him up. They were about the same height and build, minus the sagging potbelly Dope boy had as a result of years of fast food. Myra's frowned turned into a smile. Dope boy smiled as Myra grabbed him by the hand and led him to her car.

Myra parked behind Stevenson high school. The whole fifteen minutes it took to get there, Dope boy was feeling all over her. Myra smacked his hand away when he tried to slide it between her legs. Now that they were parked, Dope boy decided to slow his roll and lay his mack down.

"You're so beautiful, ma. That's word to everything I love."

Myra climbed over the armrest and started tonguing him down. Dope boy palmed Myra's butt as she straddled him. He broke the lip lock and tried to suck on her neck, but the bandana was in the way. He tried removing it from around Myra's neck; she stopped him. He stopped tugging at it and started tugging at her pants.

Myra allowed him to unbutton them and then stopped him. "You got a condom?"

"Hell fucking yeah."

"Put it on and then join me in the backseat." She tried climbing off him, but he held her in place. "We can do it right here in the front."

"I want you to hit it from the back, I like deep penetration." Myra licked his lips. Dope boy nearly shot his load. He tossed Myra off him and reached into his pocket for his condom.

Myra climbed in the back. "You got it on yet?"

"I'm rolling it on right—" His back arched as Myra looped her arm under his chin and locked in the chokehold. Dope boy growled as he clawed and then punched at Myra's arm. His eyes popped open when she cut off his air supply completely.

"I'ma kill you... bitch," he choked out. He pulled his feet onto the seat, trying to get enough leverage to flip Myra over the front seat. Myra had her knees anchored against the back of the seat; she yanked harder. Dope boy's tongue shot out his mouth as he flailed his arms and flopped like a fish. He walked his feet up the dashboard until they were pressed against the windshield and then pushed back with everything that he had.

He slid over the front seat, thinking he would land on Myra and smother her with his body weight and force her to break the hold. Myra was ready for him. She wrapped her legs around his waist and locked her ankles around his stomach as he landed, back first, on top of her.

Dope boy gritted his teeth as he tried to grind his weight against her. He tried to scream for help when he started feeling light-headed. The only sound coming from his throat was a hacking cough. He started kicking on the backdoor and slamming his arms against the seats. He went from kicking the door to trying to kick out a window, but by that time, his boots felt like they weighed fifty pounds apiece.

In a last desperate attempt, he reached back, thinking if he pulled patches of her hair out her head, she would let go. He pulled Myra's knit hat off and grabbed for her hair. A look of shock tattooed his face as he palmed her baldhead.

"Fuck," he wheezed just before losing consciousness. Myra held on, her arms burning. Twenty seconds later, she released him. She felt for his pulse; it was weak, but it was there.

She wiggled from under him and sat up. She caught her breath and then removed one of his boots and tried it on: Perfect fit.

She stripped him down to his underwear and then scanned the area to make sure the coast was clear before opening the backdoor and dumping him onto the sidewalk.

Myra climbed into the driver's seat and pulled off. She dug into her tote bag and pulled out Moon's phone and made another call to the woman she called earlier.

"Peace be upon you," Myra said in Arabic when the woman answered.

"And peace be upon you," the woman said, returning the Islamic greeting.

"There's been a change of plan," Myra said. "I need to act now."

"I saw you on the news," the woman said. "That changes things."

"The only thing it changes is our timetable."

"And what about the suitcases?"

"We have to assume that they've been found."

The woman started cursing in Arabic.

"They were only going to be used as a diversionary tactic."

"Everyone's not in place," the woman reminded Myra.

"Fuck everyone else. I don't need them; you know that."

The woman didn't answer.

"I can do this but it has to be now."

"Call back tomorrow; I'll have an answer for you then."

"I need an answer now. How long do you think I can play cat and mouse with the police?"

"I don't have the authority to give you an answer."

"Then put someone on the phone who does."

"It's not that simple."

"The Demons are in New York."

"Impossible."

Myra could hear the fear in the woman's voice. "They're here, which means, they know something is going down. The plan has to be set in motion now."

"Hold on." The woman put the phone on speaker. "Peace be upon you, Army Specialist Myra Taft."

Myra's heart fluttered as she instantly recognized the voice. "And peace be upon you."

"I can tell you're surprised to hear my voice."

"Very."

"A lot has changed since we last met. I've… how do you say it… stopped living in a fantasy world where I thought violence wasn't an option. It seems that violence is the only thing your government respects. I miss our talks, Three."

"I would love to catch up on old times, but time isn't on my side."

The conversation turned serious. "And how do you know the Demons are in New York?"

"One of them paid my psychologist a visit." Myra could hear people in the background speaking rapidly in Arabic.

"I'm sorry, Myra Taft—"

"No!" Myra shouted into the phone. "Don't do this to me. I've waited too long for this. They have to pay for what they did to me."

"And I'm sure you'll find a way to make your government pay, it just won't be with our help."

"Wait—"

The woman hung up on Myra. Myra called back three times, each time her call rolled right into voice mail. She dismantled Moon's phone and headed to Brooklyn.

Cleary pulled up to Jamie Towers. Omar's apartment was on the tenth floor.

Laura looked up at the building. "That's where she is?"

"I hope so, wait here." He got out and headed to the building. A moment later, he heard the car door slam. He turned around.

"You really didn't expect me to wait in the car, did you?"

Cleary shook his head, and just continued walking.

In the elevator on their way to the tenth floor, Cleary unbuttoned his overcoat and slid on a pair of black gloves and pulled out a Taser gun from the inside of his overcoat. He saw Laura staring at him. He gave her a faint smile.

"She might not want to come willingly."

Laura swallowed and noticed her throat was dirt-dry. *Maybe I should've stayed in the car*, she thought.

On the tenth floor, they soft-stepped it to Omar's apartment. He stopped by the door and listened. No sounds came from the apartment. He pulled out what looked like a palm-sized drill. Cleary stuck the three inch long drill bit into the lock and turned it on. The device unlocked the door immediately. Cleary pocketed the drill and drew his 9mm. from its holster.

What happened to the stun gun? Laura thought as she stared at the gun. *I really should've stayed in the car.*

"Wait here," Cleary whispered. He turned the knob and entered the apartment. He went from room to room. Myra had been here; he could feel it. He checked the closets in the bedroom. In the female closet, he noticed two empty hangers. One next to dress pants, one next to some dressy blouses. Nothing else in the room seemed to be missing. He knew she no longer had on the jeans and sweat hood the two officers said she was wearing. He put his gun away and exited the apartment.

"She was here, but she's long gone," he said to Laura, as they headed to the elevator.

"What now?"

"I'm back to square one."

They rode the elevator in silence. When they exited the building, Cleary picked up on the commotion going on across the street near the high school. Two guys were standing by a black SUV arguing with one another. What struck Cleary as odd was the fact that one of the kids was in his underwear. The kid in his underwear snatched the pile of clothes from the other guy and started putting them on. Cleary caught snippets of their conversation. He heard *bitch* and *stronger than a motherfucker.*

"Wait here," Cleary said to Laura, as he crossed the street. He heard her heels clicking after him. He didn't even bother turning around to argue with her.

Dope boy and the weed seller stopped arguing and looked toward Cleary and Laura.

Cleary pulled out his ID as he approached them. "My name is Andrew Cleary. I'm with the US Army."

"Man… go 'head," Dope boy said. "We ain't trying to hear that 'be all you can be' bullshit."

"I'm not recruiting. I overheard your conversation."

"What conversation?" the weed seller asked.

Cleary pointed at Dope boy. "The one where you were talking about a bitch being stronger than a motherfucker."

Both dealers looked at each other. Then Dope boy spoke. "I don't know where you're from soldier boy, but 'round here motherfuckers get murdered for minding other people's business, you feel me?"

Cleary held his hands up. "I don't mean to be in your business, but I believe you may have been talking about a woman I'm looking for."

Dope boy looked at his partner. "Can you believe this guy?" He then looked back at Cleary. "Maybe you don't understand what mind your business means. So let me put it a different way. Get the fuck out of here before I fuck you up."

"Listen guys—" Laura started to say.

"And who the fuck are you?" Dope boy asked.

"Can you please just help us?" Laura asked.

Dope boy grabbed his crotch. "How about helping me by—"

Cleary's fist shot out, hitting the bull's eye on Dope boy's chin. He dropped; his partner ducked into the SUV. Cleary sprinted toward the truck. He reached the truck just as the weed seller came out brandishing a gun. Cleary kept running. He kicked the truck door into the kid. The kid grunted as the door slammed into him. Cleary wrenched the gun from him and threw him to the ground.

Cleary looked up when he heard Laura scream. Dope boy was up and charging her. He yoked her up. Laura lifted her foot and brought her pointy heel down on the Dope boy's foot and then elbowed him in the ribs and broke free. He howled in pain as he grabbed at his foot and ribs at the same time.

"I'm going to fucking kill you." He charged her again.

Cleary shot him. Dope boy jerked as ninety thousand volts of electricity buzzed through his body.

"You okay?" Cleary asked Laura. She nodded while rubbing her neck. Cleary picked the weed seller off the ground and slammed him against the SUV. "The woman, where is she?"

"I don't know, man, I swear."

Cleary hit him across the cheek with the gun that he snatched from him just a moment ago. Laura called out to him, but he ignored her.

"The woman, where is she?" he asked the kid again.

"I swear, I don't know. My boy two-wayed me, saying that the dope fiend bitch had choked him out and took everything from him, including his clothes. I jumped in my ride and met him here. I keeps a couple changes of clothes in my truck for whatever."

Cleary shoved him against the truck again. Laura grabbed him by the shoulder.

"Please," she said.

Cleary let the kid go. He saw the two-way pager on the kid's hip as well as a cell phone. Cleary pointed at Dope boy who was still unconscious. "Did he have a cell phone, as well?"

The kid nodded. "Yeah, but she took it."

"What's his name?" Cleary asked.

"Trey Dog."

"His real name."

The kid stalled for a moment. Cleary took a step toward him. "Tracy Reynolds."

"Let's go," Cleary said to Laura. He dismantled the kid's gun and threw the pieces in different directions as he and Laura headed back to his car. When they got in the car, Cleary made a call. "Tracy Reynolds, Bronx, New York. Myra may be in possession of his phone. See if you can locate it and get back to me ASAP."

"You okay?" Laura asked.

"When I say wait in the car, that's exactly what it means. That thug could've really hurt you. And for the brief moment that I took my eyes off his partner to save you, his partner could've disarmed me and shot me." Cleary shook his head. "You shouldn't be here, you're a distraction."

"A distraction? You said you needed my help to find Myra."

"And I believe that you've helped me as best as you can, but there's nothing else you can do. I'm taking you home."

"Home?" Laura said surprised. "I thought we've been through this. I'm too afraid to go home."

"I'll check your apartment to make sure it's clear. Once you're inside, don't open the door for anyone."

Laura didn't respond.

"Did you hear me?"

"Yeah, whatever."

Myra parked in front of the brownstone. She got out the car, tote bag in one hand, Dope boy's clothes in the other. She unhinged the wrought-iron gate and walked down the five steps to Moon's basement apartment. Myra followed him home one night. Didn't know when she would have to pay him a visit and kill him in his sleep. Myra quickly stripped and put on Dope boy's Louis Vuitton blue jeans and dark brown thermal shirt. Both were baggy. Baggy was good. Baggy concealed curves, breasts, and weapons. Myra then slid her arms into the beige Louis Vuitton vest and pulled on the matching fitted cap and Timberlands. A pair of shades and bandana around her neck made her transformation complete.

Myra practiced her walk, gestures, and subtle movements in front of the mirror in the living room. It wouldn't be hard to pass herself off as a man. She could cloak her femininity and man-up at will. The only problem she ever had was the voice. She could get away with speaking a couple words at a time, but any more than that, and people would assume that they were talking to a dude with a little sugar in his tank. The police were looking for a woman. Which meant they wouldn't give a man a second glance. Myra found a comfortable spot on Moon's couch and decided to rest before she moved on. It would only be a matter of time before the Demons or the police found out about this place. For now, she focused on one thought—Now that the terrorist cell in New York cut her off, how was she going to make America pay for what they did to her?

Cleary pulled up to Laura's apartment building. She got out the car without a word. They rode the elevator in silence. When they arrived at her apartment, Laura opened the door and stepped to the side for Cleary to check things out. She trailed him as he checked every room thoroughly. She walked him back to the front door and was about to close it in his face, when he stopped her.

"You have my number. If you feel like you're in danger—"

"Yeah, you'll be the first person I call."

"Hey, what I said earlier about you being a distraction…"

"You were right. I was out of my element. I'm a psychiatrist. My place is in the office. Not in the hood duking it out with thugs."

"The way you stomped on his foot and elbowed him in the ribs shocked him, and me."

"Survival instincts kicked in, I guess."

"You'd make a good soldier."

"Good night, Sergeant Cleary."

Laura closed the door and waited to hear him walk away before she dug out her cell phone and tried calling the number Myra had called her from. It rolled right into voicemail. She called Myra's phone; it rolled into voicemail, as well. She dropped down onto her couch and let out a long sigh. She winced as she touched her neck and felt that it was still sensitive from when the burglar tried to choke the life out of her. Her heart fluttered as she relived the moment. If she hadn't kneed him in the groin… she shuddered as she imagined a real janitor stumbling across her mangled body in that cold staircase. *I almost died tonight.*

Now that the high-adrenaline events were over, exhaustion overwhelmed her. The sense of relief and security she felt sitting on her couch caused her to close her eyes for just a moment: A moment that would last until sunrise.

CHAPTER 6

*D*emon Three slowly regained consciousness. She felt Demon Two's hands around her neck trying to stop the bleeding.

"Strip her; we can't do anything for her." Demon Three heard Demon One say to Demon Two.

"But—" Demon Two started to protest.

"I said strip her. We have to go now."

Demon Three felt Demon Two unclipping her communications equipment, and weapons. After a few moments of silence, she tried lifting her hand up to the gaping wound in her neck. She worked up the strength to get her hand there, but she didn't have the strength to apply enough pressure to stop the bleeding. She slowed her heart rate to reduce the amount of blood that was now pooling around the back of her head, but the blood was still spilling from her neck.

She gasped when she felt a pair of hands knock hers away and wrap themselves around her neck. Myra's eyes fluttered until she focused on the person choking the life out of her—it was Jamilah. Her facial expression was craze and rage mixed as she tightened her hands around Myra's neck.

Myra stopped struggling. She was dying anyway. The least she could do was give the girl the satisfaction of killing one of the demons responsible for her mother and grandmother's murder. Myra closed her eyes and let her hand fall away from Jamilah's.

Thirty-six. The number popped into Myra's head. She had infiltrated three terrorist cells—each consisted of twelve members. She had killed all thirty-six just to locate the whereabouts of one man.

Zakawi.

The Powers That Be knew that eliminating Zakawi would deliver a blow so crippling to the terrorist network that with a few coordinated attacks by America and its allies, the war on terror would be over. Killing Zakawi would win the war on terror. But there was only one problem with that theory. Neither the United States, nor any of its allies knew what Zakawi looked like; nor did they know where to find him. All they had was a name, and the word of a few detainees in Guantanamo Bay who swore, after intense interrogation, that he did exist. But none of them knew his location. When all agencies failed to locate him or even confirm that he existed, the Secretary of Defense gave the Director of Special Ops the green light to unleash the demons. Seven months and thirty-six bodies later, the demons confirmed Zakawi's existence and where to find him.

Myra heard screaming and high-pitched cursing in Arabic. She felt Jamilah's hands being pulled from around her neck. Faces twice as crazed as Jamilah's stared down at her. She was too weak to move or speak. The pool of blood beneath her head was starting to harden.

One of the men pulled out a pistol and jammed it in her mouth. Jamilah was screaming in the background. Myra could hear what she was saying, but she couldn't understand why she was saying it. Jamilah was pleading for Myra's life.

The man with the gun in Myra's mouth looked down at her, his eyes red with rage, tears soaking his beard. He shoved the gun deeper into Myra's mouth until it hit the back of her throat and made her gag.

"Please, daddy," Myra heard Jamilah say. "She tried to stop them."

Myra focused on the face in front of her. Finally, she was face to face with the world's most elusive man.

Zakawi yelled at the top of his lungs and then pulled the gun out of Myra's mouth. Jamilah rushed back to her side and covered the wound. She begged the men standing around to help Myra. None of them moved

"Daddy, please, tell them to help her."

Zakawi stared down at the bodies of his wife and mother. He closed his eyes and gave a faint nod. One of his men pulled Jamilah away from Myra and started tending to the wound as another ran to get a first-aid kit.

Zakawi fell to his knees in front of his mother and wife and held their lifeless bodies in his arms and swore on his life that America would pay for what they've done.

Myra leaped off the couch, jumping away from shadows and swinging at them. She didn't stop tripping until she realized she was in Moon's apartment. She felt like she was suffocating. She ran to the sink and splashed water on her face. The cool water calmed her down instantly. It had been months since she dreamed of Iraq. *Fuck this,* Myra thought as she looked at herself one last time in the mirror before leaving the apartment. She might not be able to get her hands on high-grade explosives, but she could get her hands on the next best thing. "Time to go shopping."

Laura struggled to keep her eyes open the next day, as her two o' clock appointment rambled on and on about the chance of him and his ex-wife getting back together. Laura wanted to shake him by the collar and say, *Hey, stupid, she remarried and has two kids by her present husband. She's not even thinking about your sorry ass.* But instead, she took three gulps of her coffee and pretended to be listening. A soft chime sounded to let her client know that his time was up.

"See you next week, Dr. Randal."

"Yes, I'll be expecting you," Laura said with a smile. She couldn't wait for him to leave so she could kick off her shoes and take a nap. She had fallen asleep on her couch last night and didn't wake up until she heard her alarm clock in her bedroom going off. But the six hours of sleep didn't seem to do her any good. She guessed that the stress of the night's events took more of a toll on her body and mind then she assumed.

She kicked off one shoe and was just about to kick off the other when her secretary stuck her head in the door. "Dr. Randal, Sergeant Cleary is here to see you."

Laura sighed and put her shoe back on. "Send him in."

Sergeant Cleary walked in hesitantly, and didn't make eye contact with Laura until he stood in front of her desk. "May I sit?"

"It depends on what comes out of your mouth next."

Cleary clasped his hands behind his back. "About what I said last night..."

"You were right, I was in your way. You don't have to apologize."

"You weren't in my way. I was just frustrated. It was wrong for me to take my frustration out on you. Can I make it up to you? A cup of coffee maybe?"

"Any leads on Myra yet?" Laura asked, quickly changing the subject.

"Nothing yet. All I have to go on is that kid's cell phone. It's not in his name. My people are coming up with names of the kid's family members. Maybe I'll get lucky and will find the phone under one of their names." Cleary eyed the couch so many clients sat in. "May I?" he asked, pointing to the couch.

"Be my guest," Laura said with a shrug.

Sergeant Cleary ran his hand across the couch's soft leather before sitting down on it. "Wow, this is comfortable."

"The more comfortable a client is, the more inclined they will be to opening up," Laura said.

"Did this couch work for Myra? Did it help her open up?"

"She never even looked at the couch. She preferred this straight-back chair," Laura said, pointing to the chair across her desk.

"I wonder how she did it." Cleary said, as he stared at the ceiling.

"Did what?"

"Survive. She was at the mercy of those savages for three years. Three years of interrogation, three years of humiliation."

"She's lucky to be alive," Laura said.

"No, Doc, luck has nothing to do with it. Her training kept her alive, her belief kept her alive."

"Her Belief?"

"Her belief in her country and what she was fighting for."

"And what exactly was she fighting for?"

"Iraqi freedom."

Laura snorted.

Cleary sat up. "Did I say something wrong?"

Laura shook her head. "No, I'm sorry."

"Say what's on your mind, Doc."

"I just don't believe in war."

Cleary's face knotted up. "And why's that?"

Laura sat back in her chair and took off her glasses. "I'm really tired, and I have another session in about forty minutes. Maybe some other time."

"Whatever you say, Doc. But remember, Freedom has its price."

"So does war," Laura said with passion. "Thousands of American soldiers and thousands of Iraqi soldiers and civilians are paying the price with their lives. President Bush is spending a billion dollars a week on this war. Imagine the freedom we would have in our own communities if he were pumping a billion dollars a week into our inner cities. We would have freedom. Freedom from being robbed, raped, and murdered. Our kids would have the same chance at an education that kids growing up in suburban America are afforded. Our kids would want to be more than just rappers or video vixens or basketball players."

"Wow, Doc. I didn't take you for an activist."

"I'm not an activist, I'm a realist."

"Then you should know that although war can be bloody and have its tragedies, it's a necessary evil," Cleary said.

"What makes war evil is the fact that ninety percent of all wars ever fought was over land, wealth, power, or natural resources. It's the greed of a few waging war under the guise of freedom or honor or peace or to prevent some dastardly mastermind from taking over the world," Laura said with disgust.

"So you think this war is over oil?"

"It's not over weapons of mass destruction or 'Iraqi freedom'. If that's the premise we're basing our invasion on, then that means we'll be going into Iran next and then Korea."

Cleary smiled. Before he had a chance to say another word, his phone rang. "Yeah," he answered as he stood up. "I'm on my way." He ended the call. "I would love to stay and chat, Doc, but we finally tracked down the phone. The kid had it turned on in his aunt's name. Myra's in Brooklyn."

Laura stood up. "Wait."

Cleary stopped in his tracks. "This can get real complicated, Doc."

"I'm a psychiatrist; I specialize in complicated."

"Sorry, Doc, not this time." Cleary shot out the door.

Laura sat back down and kicked off her shoes. She sighed when her cell phone rang. The number came up as blocked. "Hello?"

"Hey, Doc."

Laura sat up in her chair. "Myra?"

"Did I catch you at a bad time?"

"No, are you all right?"

Myra snorted a line of dope. "Haven't been all right in a long time."

"Myra, I can help you work this out."

"It's beyond help. My life is over."

"Don't say that."

"It is. My life was over three years ago when my team left me to die."

"Your medical condition is documented," Laura said. "I can personally testify that you weren't in your right state of mind that day at your apartment."

Myra started humming an unfamiliar tune. "Do you believe in demons, Doc?"

"Excuse me?"

"Demons. Do you believe in them?"

"Yes... I also believe in angels."

Myra chuckled. "Didn't know you were religious, Doc."

"I said I believe. Belief and religion are two different things."

"Good point, Doc. So tell me, what's the difference between an angel and a demon?"

Laura thought about it for a moment. "Well... very simply put, demons serve themselves; angels serve others."

"I served my country, but I'm far from an angel."

"Myra, just because you may have done some bad things in the name of war—"

"Bad is putting it lightly. I've done things for my country that I'm too ashamed to ever mention." Myra snorted another line of dope. "You really want to know the difference between angels and demons, Doc?"

"I'm listening."

"Angels do what's right; demons do what needs to be done."

"Myra—"

"Don't waste your breath, Doc. I know what I am and I'm okay with it."

"You can call yourself whatever you want, but I feel in my heart that you're not a bad person."

"Never trust your heart, Doc. Your heart will get you killed."

"I'm not your husband, I won't abandon you. Let me help you."

Laura could hear Myra trying to muffle her sobs. "Tell me where you are. I'll come alone, we'll figure this out... together."

"Doc, God be my witness, if you betray me, I will make you die a thousand deaths."

"Myra, please tell me where you are."

"380 West 125th Street. There's an abandoned fried chicken spot on the corner." Myra ended the call.

Laura stared at her phone, debating on whom to call. Should she call Cleary, Jennings, or... A tear escaped the corner of her eye as she dialed a number from memory.

"Yes," the man answered.

"She called me."

"And?"

"She gave me an address, she wants me to meet her there." The man didn't answer. "What should I do?"

"Meet her," the man said.

"And then what?" Laura asked. The man ended the call. Laura sighed as she grabbed her purse and headed for the door. She stopped and made one last call. "Yes, I need to speak with Major Jennings, please."

By the time Laura arrived at the abandoned chicken spot, the sun was down and the streetlights were on. She parked across the street where she had a clear view of the boarded up restaurant. She got out of her car and looked up and down the block. Someone turned the corner. Laura watched him as he walked past the abandoned chicken spot and crossed the street and started heading straight for her.

Laura swallowed the fear rising in her throat, as the man seemed to quicken his pace toward her. Laura was about to jump back into her car when the guy removed his cap and she saw the baldhead.

"Myra?" Laura caught a shadow shooting out of a dark doorway. "Myra lookout!"

Myra turned, but it was too late. The janitor who nearly killed Laura yesterday lowered his head and hit Myra like a battering ram. Myra and the man flew onto the hood of a car. As they slid off, the man threw a flurry of punches. Myra blocked them easily and threw a well-timed, well-aimed punch of her own. The force of the blow nearly crushed his larynx. He staggered back, coughing. Myra followed up with a front kick to his lower stomach, bending him over, then she brought her

knee up to connect with his nose. Just before her knee connected, the man brought his hands up to take the brunt of the blow.
He reached out to grab Myra, but she was already moving. She
spun to her right and caught him behind the ear with a spinning
heel kick. The man fell shoulder first into the car he slammed
her on top of earlier. He saw Myra preparing for another front
kick and dove out of the way. Myra's foot slammed into the
door where his head was a split second ago. The man hopped
back to his feet and intensified his attack. He launched faster
punches; harder kicks, trying to go over and under Myra's
defensive blocks.

Myra's hands and arms weaved defensive circles with such
speed and precision that only a few blows penetrated, none of
which hit her flush. She would cut a circle short every now and
then and snap off a stiff-fingered jab to his eyes or throat to
which he blocked or dodged.

Laura watched the exchange in awe. The man had gotten
the jump on Myra but she quickly evened things up and it
looked like she was about to end it. Or so Laura thought.

The man feinted with a straight right to Myra's midsection
and then came over her defenses with a left hook to her jaw.
Myra stumbled back against the car, eyes fluttering, arms
dropping to her sides.

"You were always a sucker for the left hook," the man
snarled, and then rushed her. His knockout blow was aimed at
the bridge of her nose. Myra waited until he was fully committed to the punch before dropping to one knee and driving his
balls into his stomach.

"And you were always a sucker for the one playing possum." Myra was huffing and could barely keep her eyes open. *Fucking dope*, she thought. *It's a miracle I lasted this long.*

Instead of the man going down, he charged Myra and slammed her into the car once, twice, three times; leaving her breathless.

Myra saw him reaching into his pocket, but she didn't have the strength to stop him. He pulled out his gun and jammed it under her chin. "See you in hell, Taft." The man gasped as a pair of arms wrapped around his neck and cut off his air supply. Laura had jumped on his back. "Ahhh!" the man yelled as Laura bit down on his ear. Myra moved the gun from under her chin a split second before it went off.

Laura held on to the man as he screamed and tried flipping her off his back. He backed into the car. Laura loosened her grip and the man was able to flip her off. She landed butt-first onto the pavement. She spat at him and looked up at him defiantly.

He pointed his gun at her and pulled the trigger. Myra kicked his hand as the gun fired, sending the bullet sailing over Laura's head. Myra judo flipped him and ripped the gun from his hand. She pointed it at him.

"Looks like you'll be going to hell before me."

"Taft!"

Myra looked up. Cleary was running towards her, gun out, firing. Myra dove over the car for cover, while firing three shots at him.

"Sergeant Cleary," Laura yelled. "What the hell are you—"

He yanked her off the ground and pulled her in front of himself. Myra popped her head over the hood and took aim but she didn't fire.

"Sweetheart," Cleary said mockingly. "I've missed you."

"I've missed you, too," Myra said. "All three times."

"Aim isn't what it used to be, huh? Especially with the dope in your system." Laura struggled in Cleary's grip. The janitor got to his feet and pulled a gun from behind his back.

Cleary and the man opened fire at Myra. She ducked and ran alongside the cars until she reached the Malibu. Myra opened the door.

"Taft!" Cleary called out. "You get in that car, I'll put a bullet in her head." He pressed his gun harder against Laura's head.

"Go ahead. See if I care."

Laura's eyes widened. Cleary and his partner turned their heads when they heard engines racing up the block toward them. The headlights from the two SUVs were on them from both ends of the block. Myra jumped in her car and waited for the SUV to drive past her before she slapped the car in reverse and backed out of the block and took off. The SUV that drove past her backed up and took off after her.

Major Jennings and two soldiers climbed out of their SUV to confront Cleary and his partner. Jennings locked eyes with Cleary. "I'm ordering you to stand down and surrender your weapons to my men."

"You know we can't do that."

"I am giving you a direct order to—"

"Your pay grade isn't high enough to give us orders, Major." Cleary shoved Laura toward him and then him and his partner aimed their guns at the two soldiers who were aiming their guns at them. "We're going to leave now, Major," Cleary said.

"I can't let you do that."

"It's either that or you're going to have a bloody mess to explain."

Major Jennings clenched his jaw and looked at his men. "Lower your weapons." His soldiers didn't budge. "I said lower your weapons."

Cleary smiled when the soldiers put their guns away. He winked at the Major. "I advise you to mind your business, Major. Taft is no longer your concern." Cleary and his partner got into Cleary's car and drove off.

"Are you okay?" Jennings asked Laura.

"What in the hell just happened?"

"Nothing," Jennings said, "in comparison to what's about to happen."

CHAPTER 7

L aura sat in an office in the back of the Army recruiting center. The only furniture in the room was a table and two chairs. After she told Major Jennings all about the man who identified himself as Sergeant Cleary and about the break in, the Major left the room and came back a few minutes later with two cups of coffee, a box of donuts, and a manila folder. He placed a cup in front of her and sipped from his.

"I'm sorry you got dragged into this," he said.

"And what exactly did I get dragged into, Major?"

Jennings opened the box of donuts. "Would you care for one?"

"My office was broken into, I was attacked, I was in the company of a man who claimed to be Myra's husband, which I'm starting to believe was a lie." Laura threw her hands in the air. "It's all lies, all of it. Keep your donuts, what I want is the truth."

Jennings choked on his donut. "The truth? The truth is subject to change, Doc. Today's truth can very well be tomorrow's lie. I can't tell you the truth, but I'll do even better. I'll tell you what you're not supposed to know."

"This is bullshit, I'm leaving."

"You know I can't let you leave. If I let you walk out of here, Myra will kill you before sunrise."

"And why would she do that?"

Major Jennings opened the folder and read from a transcript of a recorded phone call. "Doc, God be my witness. If you betray me, I will make you die a thousand deaths."

Laura's eyes widened. "You're tapping my phone?"

"I knew she would call you sooner or later."

Laura took a deep breath and then exhaled. The air coming out of her nose could boil water. "You have no authority to hold me." She stood up. "I'm out of here."

"Sit down, Doctor."

"Fuck you."

Jennings sipped his coffee and waited for Laura to put her hand on the knob before he spoke. "Myra Taft, aka Maya Taft, aka Mia Taft, aka Mary Taft."

Laura removed her hand from the knob.

Jennings continued. "No matter what name she goes by, one thing remains the same."

"And what's that?" Laura asked.

"She's the deadliest woman I know." He looked at the empty seat across from him and then looked back to Laura. She didn't move from the door. "Oh stop it, Laura, you know you want to hear what I have to say."

"Only if it's the truth."

Jennings smiled. "I'll tell you what you're not supposed to know."

Laura looked at the door and then looked back at him. As she weighed her options, she got the eerie feeling that she was about to make a deal with the devil. She slowly walked back to the chair and sat down. "The man who was passing himself off as her husband wasn't really her husband, was he?"

"Nope. But as much as they fought and argued, you would think they were husband and wife."

"Is he going to kill her?"

"Yes."

"Why?" Laura asked.

"Because that's what he does. He does what no one else can do. So does Myra, and so does Walker."

"Walker?"

"The janitor impersonator."

"So they all used to work together?"

Jennings finished off his coffee and donut and then wiped his mouth with a napkin. "The woman you know as Myra Taft belonged to an elite unit that is highly classified."

"How elite?" Laura asked.

"There were only three of them."

"How classified?"

"They don't exist."

"So, they're like superspies or something?" Laura said sarcastically.

"No, they're terrorists."

"What?"

"In case you haven't noticed, we're at war. And it's not with a country or with Islam. We're at war with an ideology. Terrorism."

Laura finally sat down.

Jennings continued. "A war against terrorism cannot be fought with conventional tactics. Terrorism doesn't respect the rules of engagement or the agreements reached under the Geneva Convention. Terrorism only respects one thing. Terror."

Laura didn't realize it, but she was shaking her head in disbelief. But Jennings continued. "Myra's team was trained to win the war against terror. Each one handpicked, each one highly intelligent, mentally and physically battle-hardened, and a naturally gifted chameleon. Given six months, any one of them could learn a country's language, history, customs, and then assimilate themselves into the societal fabric. Their mission was to infiltrate terror cells and destroy them from the inside-out."

"Army-trained terrorists," Laura said in disbelief. "Wait, why are you telling me about a unit that's not supposed to exist?"

Jennings smiled as he opened the folder and pulled out the confidentiality agreement she signed. At that moment, Laura realized that she wasn't making a deal with the devil, she already had the day she signed that agreement.

"If you divulge any of this to the public, they will write you off as a nut case, and with this signed agreement, I will put you in a padded room… for the rest of your life."

Laura started to feel nauseated. "Besides shutting me up, why are you telling me all this?"

"You heard what Cleary told me tonight. He told me to mind my business. Well, I can't do that. Myra is my business. For me, she's not just a soldier. I handpicked her. She agreed to be part of the team, because she worshipped the ground I walked on. I knew Myra from when she was a teenager. Her father was the best goddamned soldier I had the pleasure of serving with."

"Had?" Laura said.

"He's dead. Died in Desert Storm. Killed by friendly fire. A wet behind the ear soldier with a jittery trigger finger."

Laura shook her head. "That's awful."

"Myra took it hard. She would've taken it better if he was killed by the enemy, but to be killed by one of your own…"

"War is so evil," Laura said, clenching her fist. "So that made her join the Army?"

"Not really," Major Jennings said. "She started acting out. Violence, drugs, in and out of trouble. I stepped in and convinced her to join the Army. She needed an outlet for the rage that was building up inside her."

"So, you're blaming yourself for what happened to her when she was held prisoner for all those years."

Jennings looked at her surprised that she knew about Myra's imprisonment.

"Cleary or whatever his name told me that. Was that a lie, as well?"

"No. Three years later, a patrol found her wandering in the desert dehydrated and hallucinating." Jennings stopped talking, but Laura heard when his voice began to crack. "I was so happy to have her back that I did whatever she wanted me to do."

"All the way down to letting her choose her own psychiatrist."

Jennings nodded. "I thought it would be good for her you know, to talk to someone who wasn't Army."

Laura reached for the Styrofoam cup of coffee; her hand was shaking. She gulped down the warm coffee, and then folded her arms across her chest and avoided eye contact. "So, now what?"

"I could let you go, use you as bait, wait for Myra to come after you, and then pray that I can capture her before she kills you."

"Or…" Laura said.

"Or…" Jennings pulled out some photographs from the folder and placed them in front of Laura. "Anyone look familiar? A client or ex client maybe."

Laura looked at all the pictures. They looked like they were taking by a surveillance team, because every one captured the person crossing the street or getting into a car or walking into a restaurant. The men and women looked to be of Middle Eastern descent. Laura shook her head. "I don't recognize any of them."

"They all have two things in common," Major Jennings said. "All of them are of Middle Eastern descent, and two…" he pointed out a person that was in each picture.

Laura didn't see it before, but now she did. The woman who was crossing the street. Myra was waiting for her on the other side. The man who was getting into the car, Myra was in the backseat. And the two women who were walking into the restaurant, Myra was already sitting at one of the tables.

"I don't believe in coincidences, Doctor."

"I know what this could look like, but you can't just assume that these people are terr—"

"Then there's this." Jennings said, pulling out two more photos. The first was of two suitcases found in the basement of Myra's apartment building. "These are suitcase nukes."

The blood drained from Laura's face.

"Each could produce a blast that could kill hundreds instantly, and thousands more after the initial blast."

"How could Myra... how could something like this even get into the country, Major?"

"Contrary to popular belief, the United States can't catch every bomb or nuke that enters the country." Major Jennings showed Laura the last picture. "This is the inside of the abandon chicken shack."

Laura could make out what looked like boxes of bleach, cleansers, and detergents. "It looks like cleaning supplies," Laura said.

"To civilians, they are cleaning supplies. To a demon trained in toxicology, the right mixture would produce a toxic liquid with the acidity level that would blister skin upon contact, and whose fumes, if inhaled, would attack the nervous system and cause cardiac arrest in under five minutes."

"Oh my God. Myra's trying to... to... commit a terrorist attack on U.S. soil?" Laura's brain started to feel numb as she tried to process what was going on. "Cleary and Walker..."

"They have their orders. They have no intention on bringing her in alive. Now, you know why it's important that I find her before they do."

"And how are you going to do that?"

Jennings looked at her.

"No. Hell no. Is this what this whole conversation was about?"

Jennings didn't speak.

"You were going to use me for bait from the get-go."

"I would rather you volunteer for this mission."

"Volun what? Mission? I'm not in the Army. I'm a civilian. I'm not volunteering for anything."

"Like you said, I have no authority to hold you," Jennings said with a shrug. "You're free to go."

Laura's mouth dropped open. "I don't believe this. What if Myra kills me before you get a chance to capture her?"

"I'm sorry, Doctor."

"Sorry my ass!" Laura swiped the photographs, empty cups, and box of donuts off the table and headed out the door.

CHAPTER 8

*I*raq three years ago…

Days slipped into weeks. Weeks meshed into months. Myra tried to keep track of how long she had been held prisoner, but the brutal sessions of interrogation intensified when she wouldn't cooperate, causing her to blackout for days at a time. Every time she came to, she would be in a different location. For the past few days, she was tucked away in one of the thousands of caves that dotted the mountainside. Myra struggled against the chains that held her stretched across a slab of rock; she knew that no rescue team was coming for her and she knew the only reason she was still alive was because she hadn't given up any information, yet. Enduring the torture sessions were her only way of staying alive and finding a way out of the chains that never came off her ankles and wrists.

Myra worked herself to exhaustion struggling against the bulky chains. She lay on the slab of rock breathing hard. She stopped breathing when she heard a footstep scrape the ground She sighed and relaxed when she felt the warm, damp rag on her forehead. There was only one person who was permitted to tend to her.

Once a week, for the past eight months, Zakawi allowed Jamilah to come to wherever they were holding Myra so she could bathe her. Myra was never given the decency to relieve herself in private. Whatever rock she was stretched across and chained down to was where she relieved herself. And Jamilah would have to clean up after her. Myra realized that Zakawi wasn't only humiliating her with such treatment, but cleaning up piss and shit was the price Jamilah had to pay for begging her father not to kill Myra.

Jamilah's lack of violence angered Zakawi. No matter how much he tried to turn her into a fighter, she would rebel and tell him that she wanted to be a doctor; that she wanted to save lives, not take them. That night when he saw Myra lying in his living room bleeding out, he knew she was one of the American dogs his people referred to as the Demons. He could see it in her eyes. She lay there dying and she wasn't afraid. He stuck his gun in her mouth and she welcomed it. And here was his daughter begging for the life of a worthless animal who just butchered her mother and grandmother. Zakawi granted her wish, for the time being, but as long as Myra remained alive, it would be Jamiliah's job to clean up after the animal.

Jamilah continued to dab at Myra's forehead with the soapy rag. She then ran it across Myra's lips. Jamilah jumped back when Myra bit down on the rag and wretched it from her hand. Myra sucked the soapy water out of the rag like it was spring water. Jamilah quickly regained her composure and fought Myra for the rag. She ripped it from Myra's mouth just as Hassan stepped into view with his AK47 aimed at Myra.

"What?" Jamilah said to him in an irritated tone.

"I heard noises."

"I'm fine."

Hassan looked at the chains securing Myra's hands and wrists before lowering his weapon. "I'm just outside," he said to Jamilah.

"You're always just outside."

"Water," Myra croaked.

"You almost got me in trouble," Jamilah whispered harshly. She made sure Hassan was gone before she pulled a water skin from under her long dress. Zakawi had Myra on a strict diet. He made sure she was only given enough food and water to stay alive. Myra lost thirty-two pounds in the first two months. Now, at ninety-eight pounds, she was nothing but skin and skeleton.

Jamilah twisted the cap off the water skin. She poured water into Myra's mouth until it was empty.

"More," Myra whispered.

"There is no more."

Myra slowly turned her head to the bucket of soapy water.

"What am I going to bathe you with?"

"I don't need a bath."

Jamilah scrunched up her nose. "Yes, you do." From day one, Myra was stripped of her fatigues. Her only clothing was two sheets. One wrapped around her upper body, the other around her lower body. Jamilah held her breath and began unwrapping the top sheet. Myra winced. Jamiliah could see the chains biting into Myra's wrists.

"Hassan!"

A moment later, Hassan walked into the cave.

Jamilah pointed to the chains around Myra's wrists. "Removed these so I can bathe her properly."

"Your father said—"

"My father's not here. Look at her wrists." Jamilah showed him the black and blue bruises. "This is not Islam. This is not how prisoners are supposed to be treated. You know this."

Hassan looked around.

"Hassan!"

He flinched at the sound of his name. He took the key ring off his belt and tossed it to her. "Just her wrists, Jamilah." He kept his AK pointed at Myra.

Jamilah unlocked the chains. Myra was stretched out on the slab for so long that she couldn't move her arms. Jamilah had to bring them down to her sides for her. Jamilah cut her eyes at Hassan as she continued unwrapping Myra's top sheet, exposing her stomach. Hassan immediately averted his gaze.

"I can't bathe her with you watching," Jamilah said to Hassan.

"I'm not leaving you here with her unchained."

"Fine." Jamilah removed the top sheet completely, exposing Myra's breasts.

"Allah forgive me," Hassan said and turned his back. "I'll be right outside. Call me when you're done."

Jamilah smiled and then helped Myra sit up. Jamilah looked down at the chains on Myra's feet. "I will free your feet if you promise not to try and escape."

Myra squinted. *This girl couldn't be this naïve.* "I promise."

Jamilah unlocked the chains and helped Myra stand. Myra moaned as she felt the pins and needles throughout her whole body. She had been chained to the slab of rock for three days. She stopped feeling her limbs yesterday. Now, the blood was working its way through her limbs.

"Can you stand on your own?" Jamilah asked her.

Myra kept her arm around Jamilah and shook her head.

"Try to walk a little." Jamilah took baby steps. Myra shuffled her bare feet but couldn't keep up. "I can't."

Jamilah walked her back to the slab and sat her down. "Can you wash yourself?" Jamilah handed her the rag.

Myra grabbed it and could barely wipe the feces off her legs. That menial task left her exhausted and breathing hard.

"Are you okay?" Jamilah asked.

"Why do you do this?" Myra asked between taking deep breaths.

"Do what?"

"Take care of me."

"Would you rather someone like Hassan do this?"

"Yes."

Jamilah looked hurt. She snatched the rag from Myra and picked up the bucket.

"Wait," Myra pleaded. "I didn't mean that. I just want to know how you can be in the same room with me after what I've done. I killed your mother and grandmother.

Jamilah put the bucket down. "No, you didn't. The other demons did."

"But..." Myra struggled to speak. "I'm one of them."

"If you were one to them, you wouldn't have stopped that demon from..." Jamilah shuddered at the thought of what

103

Demon One was going to do to her with the chair leg. "Why did you stop him?"

Myra bent down and reached in the bucket for the rag. "I don't know."

"Liar."

Myra ignored her as she tried to run the rag under her arms.

"You talk in your sleep," Jamilah whispered.

"So."

"The things you say are not good. You talk about killing people."

Myra stopped wiping herself and looked at her.

"What?" Jamilah asked.

"If I make it out of here, I'm going to find the ones who left me for dead. I'm going to rock them to sleep and then I'm going to kill them."

"What do you mean 'rock them to sleep?'"

Zakawi smiled when he heard Myra's last statement. Hassan was so into his cigarette that he didn't see Zakawi when he was ascending the mountain. Hassan nearly pissed himself when he and Zakawi entered the cave and he saw that Jamilah had freed Myra completely. Zakawi grabbed Hassan by the collar and stepped just inside the cave where he could see Myra and hear Myra and Jamilah's conversation. After he heard Myra's last statement about killing the ones who left her for dead, he ran into view.

"Jamilah!"

Jamilah jumped to her feet. "Daddy, I was just—"

Zakawi closed the distance between them and slapped her. "Are you out of your mind?"

Myra threw the soapy rag in Zakawi's face and charged him. She felt as if she ran into a brick wall. She crumbled at his feet. Zakawi laughed and then kicked her.

"Daddy, no, it's my fault. I unchained her."

Zakawi glared at Jamilah and then yelled for Hassan.

"I am here," Hassan said.

"Chain the animal back up, now!"

Hassan picked Myra off the ground and slammed her back onto the slab

of rock so hard it made Jamilah cringe. Myra tried to struggle against Hassan, but she didn't have the strength left in her. Once Hassan snapped the pad locks closed, he stood at attention. Zakawi slapped him twice.

"The next time I see her out of her chains, you will be taking her place on that slab. Am I understood?"

"Yes, yes, I understand," Hassan stammered out.

"Wait outside," Zakawi said to him. When Hassan left, Zakawi grabbed the front of Jamilah's dress and raised his hand to slap her.

"Hey," Myra strained to say.

Zakawi stopped in mid-swing.

"I tricked her into releasing me."

Zakawi screwed up his face. "You tricked her?"

"Yes," Myra swallowed. "She's naïve, it wasn't hard to do."

Zakawi shoved Jamilah. "Go home!" Jamilah ran out of the cave. Zakawi walked up beside Myra and stared down at her naked body. He looked down at the bucket of soapy water and then to the rag she threw at him. He picked up the rag and covered Myra's face with it and then poured the bucket of soapy water over the rag. The water running into Myra's mouth and nose tricked her brain into thinking she was drowning. Myra's body buck as her brain sent distress signals to every part of her body. Myra didn't stop bucking against the slab until Zakawi removed the rag.

She gasped for air while spitting up. Zakawi scrunched up his nose when he smelt the fresh shit that shot out of Myra. It ran down the side of the rock followed by a stream of hot urine.

Zakawi covered his nose with a perfumed handkerchief and then whispered in Myra's ear. "If you harm a hair on my daughter, I will do this to you for the rest of your life." He hawked up a glob of spit and spat in her face. He looked down at Myra one last time before leaving "American devil. You will tell me what I want to know, and then I will kill you."

Myra turned her head and closed her eyes. She waited until she was certain that she was alone and then she cried.

One week later, Jamilah entered the abandoned basement of the mosque where Zakawi had Myra moved. The link chain that bounded Myra's hands had been fastened onto an overhead beam. Myra's punishment for the week was to stand on her feet until her legs gave out; then she would have to hang by her arms until the pain became so unbearable that she would have to stand to take the pressure off her arms. When Jamilah walked in, Myra was standing in feces and urine, her knees buckling.

"This is how you do me?" Myra was delirious and talking to the wall. "I did what you wanted. I found him. If it weren't for me, you'd still think he was just a myth. And this is how you repay me? You leave me to die?" Myra's screeching voice sounded like nails raking down a chalkboard. Jamilah shuddered. Her eyes widened when Myra fixed her gaze on her.

"What are you looking at?" Myra's legs gave out, forcing her arms to support her weight.

Jamilah ran up the stairs and returned with Hassan.

"I can't bathe her like this."

"You heard what your father said the last time I allowed you to take the chains off."

"I'm not asking you to remove the chains; just let her arms down."

"Jamilah—"

"My father won't be back until tomorrow. He won't know."

Hassan scratched his head.

"Hassan, please."

"Okay, okay." He held his breath as he unhooked the chain from the overhead beam and dragged Myra to a pillar. He unlocked one of the cuffs so he could wrap the chain around the pillar and then he put the cuff back on her wrist. "Hurry up and bathe her so I can hang her back up." He hurried back upstairs to get back to his post.

Jamilah waited a few minutes before pulling the canteen from under her dress, and handed it to Myra. Myra didn't' have to strength to stop it from slipping out of her hands. Jamilah caught it before it hit the ground and put it to Myra's lips. Myra gulped down the water until she started choking. The last time Jamilah saw Myra she was nothing but skin and skeleton. Now, she was just skeleton.

Jamilah pulled out a baggie of meat. Myra's eyes locked onto the baggie. Jamilah could see Myra's heart beating faster, literally. She unwrapped the meat and placed it in front of Myra's mouth. She quickly yanked her hand back as Myra's neck snapped forward. Myra chomped down on the meat, chewing, sucking it. Jamilah continued to hand-feed her until it was gone.

Jamilah started to pick out the debris in Myra's matted afro. "Your hair has grown in beautifully."

Myra leaned back against the pillar and closed her eyes.

"You have beautiful hair," Jamilah said.

Myra didn't answer.

Jamilah removed the two sheets covering Myra and brought the bucket of soapy water to her side. She began wiping Myra's arms. "You lied to my father last week."

Myra opened her eyes.

"You told him you tricked me into removing your chains. Why'd you lie?"

"I don't know."

"Liar."

Myra closed her eyes.

"Hatred is consuming you."

Myra slowly opened her eyes. "Hatred is what's keeping me alive. Hatred for those who used me... hatred for those who abandoned me... and hatred for your father."

"Do you hate me?" Jamilah averted Myra's gaze as she waited for an answer.

"Yes, I hate you."

Jamilah bit her bottom lip, trying to stop the tears from falling, but she couldn't stop them. She hastily started to wrap the clean sheets around Myra.

"Did I hurt your feelings, little girl?"

"I'm not a little girl, I'm seventeen."

"And you're a cry baby; look at you," Myra taunted.

Jamilah gathered up the bucket and soiled sheets and left without saying a word.

"And don't come back," Myra yelled after her.

A few moments later, Hassan came down the stairs. "What did you say to her?"

Myra didn't respond.

Hassan uncuffed her and hung her chains back on the overhead beam. He grabbed Myra's bony face in his hand and squeezed. "What did you say to her?"

"Fuck you," Myra mumbled between her squished lips. Hassan kicked the breath out of her lungs and then covered her nose and mouth with his hand so she couldn't get any air into her deflated chest. Myra squirmed like a worm on a hook. Hassan didn't remove his hand until she was on the verge of passing out.

Myra was too busy sucking in air to notice Hassan drawing back his fist. He punched her in the center of her forehead, knocking her unconscious.

When Myra came to, she felt as if her head had been split in half. She put her weight on her feet and groaned as she felt as if her shoulders had been dislocated from supporting her weight for so long. Her wrists were swollen and purple. She knew it was nighttime because the temperature had dropped considerably. Hassan made sure she would freeze. He had unwrapped her sheets from her body and left her to stand, and hang, butt naked. Myra shivered so hard she felt as if her bones were going to crack. She couldn't take the pain and cold; she had to do something about it.

"Hassan!" she yelled his name over and over, but he didn't come down the stairs. "I know you're up there." No response. "What are you doing, jerking off? I bet you're jerking off while thinking about Jamilah. I see the way you look at her."

Hassan flew down the stairs. Myra smiled. He grabbed her by the throat.

"Stop talking like that."

"Ah, so you do want to rip her clothes off and—"

Hassan hauled off and punched Myra in the head, knocking her out. Myra got what she wanted. She wouldn't feel any pain from the cold for the rest of the night.

The next morning, Myra heard footsteps descending the basement steps. Zakawi stopped on the bottom step and stared at her. Myra locked eyes with him, refusing to feel the shame of being naked and helpless. He walked around her, inspecting her, not in a lustful way, but more like a scientist would a lab rat. He stopped walking and stood in front of her. "I am a very patient man, but I am afraid my patience has run out with you." He looked at Myra waiting for a reaction, but she didn't give him one. "Hassan has convinced me that you were nothing but a soldier sent here to kill or be killed; that your government had no reason to tell you anything of importance. Your government even denies your very existence. I should've killed you that night in my home."

"It's not too late. Put the gun to my head and pull the trigger."

"You would like that, wouldn't you?" Zakawi touched her ribs. "No, a bullet to the head is too merciful." Zakawi drew back his fist and drove it into Myra's ribs. Myra yelled out as she felt two of her ribs crack. "No demon, you will not die a quick death or an honorable one." He drew his fist back and punched her again in the ribs, cracking another one.

Myra cried out in pain.

"Hassan!" Zakawi yelled.

Hassan ran down the basement steps. "Yes."

"Take her out into the desert tonight. Make sure the wild dogs pick her bones clean."

"Yes, Zakawi."

Zakawi looked Myra over one last time. "Filthy demon." He drew his fist back and punched her on the side of the head, knocking her out.

CHAPTER 9

W hen Myra came to, she was lying on her stomach with her hands chained behind her back. She coughed and immediately regretted it. Pain shot through her broken ribs. She curled into a ball. That's when she realized three things. One, someone had wrapped Ace bandages around her ribs; two, she was no longer in the abandoned mosque basement, she was in another basement; and three, someone slipped her into a pair of tattered jeans that were five sizes too big. Myra felt someone behind her, but she was in too much pain to turn around.

"This is a bad idea," Myra heard Hassan saying. "If your father finds out that I disobeyed him, he will saw my head off with a butter knife."

"He won't find out," Jamilah said. "No one will, I promise. Allah will reward you for your mercy."

"I didn't do it for mercy."

"I know." Jamilah touched his cheek. She pulled her hand away when she heard Myra moan. She walked around to face Myra and bent down beside her. "Help me sit her up," she said to Hassan.

They each grabbed Myra under one of her arms and sat her up. Jamilah removed the lid off a bowl and spoon-fed Myra some food. After Myra swallowed a couple mouthfuls, Jamilah opened a bottle of painkillers and shook a couple into her hand.

She put them in Myra's mouth and gave her some water to help swallow them.

"I have to get back," Hassan said.

"Go, I'll be fine."

Hassan didn't like the idea of Jamilah being alone with Myra.

"I said go."

Hassan picked up his gun and left.

Myra looked around the cluttered basement. Books were strewn all over. Broken chairs and desks were piled up in each corner of the basement. "This looks like a school basement."

"It is," Jamilah said. "I used to go to this school before the war. Marines rode through in their big jeeps with their big guns mounted on top of them and destroyed everything."

"Why am I here?" Myra asked.

"My father ordered Hassan to take you out to the desert and feed you to the wild dogs. I convinced Hassan to bring you here."

"Why?"

"I was to graduate this year and then go on to the University to study medicine. My dream was to become a doctor and practice medicine in America."

"You don't speak a lick of English."

"In my class, we were learning the English alphabet before the war started." Jamilah stuck her chin out and recited the English alphabet.

"Whoopie, you know your ABCs," Myra taunted.

"I saved your life; so you will teach me English. That way when I attend the University, I can focus all of my attention on my medical degree."

The pain in Myra's ribs only allowed her to squeeze out a chuckle.

"Why are you laughing?" Jamilah asked.

"Because you're joking, right?"

"I am not joking. Hassan and I would be in serious trouble if my father knew you were still alive. You will do this for me or else—"

"Or else what?"

"I will let Hassan feed you to the dogs."

"Good," Myra said, surprising Jamilah. "Then my life of hell will be over."

"I cleaned your shit and piss, I snuck you food and water, yet you told me you hate me. Yet, I convinced Hassan to spare your life. I know you really don't want to die. What you really want is revenge. Am I right?"

Myra just stared at her.

"Teach me English, and I will release you."

"Bullshit," Myra spat out.

"I swear by Allah, I will release you so that you can take your revenge on those who abandoned you."

Myra studied Jamilah's eyes for any signs of deceit, and then looked around the basement. "This is where I will be staying?"

"Yes."

"Who else besides you and Hassan knows that I'm down here?"

"No one. Everyone knows that this was where my father used to have his meetings and store his cache of weapons. No one will dare come down here."

"What about your father?"

Jamilah shook her head. "He will never step foot back in this town; not after that night you and your demons entered our lives and changed them forever."

Myra moaned as she took a deep breath. The painkillers were finally kicking in.

"What is your answer?" Jamilah asked.

Myra dropped her head into her chest.

"I'm a quick learner." Jamilah tried not to sound desperate, but she couldn't help it.

Myra looked at her. "I'll teach you English on one condition."

"What is that?"

"I want food, lots of food; and I want all the water I can drink; and I want clothes that fit—"

"That's three conditions."

"No, that's one condition with four parts."

"Food, water, clothes. That's three."

"This is the fourth. "Myra looked at the chains. "These come off."

Jamilah shook her head. "That is not possible."

"And you want me to believe that you will release me when I'm done teaching you English. The only way I will trust you is

116

if you trust me." Myra waited for a response. "Look at me." She pointed to her emaciated body. "I probably weigh ninety pounds, I have broken ribs, and I'm too weak to do anything. You have my word as a soldier, I will not leave until I fulfill my part of the deal."

Jamilah thought about it for a moment before responding. "I will speak with Hassan."

The next morning, Jamilah entered the basement carrying a box. Hassan was close behind her with a sack slung over his shoulder. Myra kept one eye on the box and one eye on Hassan. Myra's nose twitched as the food's aroma dance in her nostrils. The eye on Hassan joined the other. Both were now on the box.

Jamilah placed the box in front of Myra and gave Hassan a head nod. He subtly shook his head and reluctantly removed the chains from Myra's ankles and wrists. Myra tried to conceal her joy, but a smile had already leaped onto her face.

"I've spoken with Hassan," Jamilah said. "He will not put the chains back on, but he has two conditions of his own."

"I'm listening," Myra said.

"He will remain by my side when I am down here with you and you will keep a distance of ten feet from us, always."

"What's the second condition?"

"When we leave, Hassan will lock the basement door."

"What if a fire breaks out down here?"

"If a fire breaks out down here, it is because you started it," Hassan shot back. "And in that case, you will have no one to blame for your death but yourself."

Myra stood up. Hassan stepped in front of Jamilah.

"Relax, Romeo."

"My name's Hassan."

Myra shook her head. "Yes, of course." Myra walked the length of the basement to get the blood in her arms and legs circulating.

"Do you agree to the conditions?" Jamilah asked.

Myra nodded, but her eyes were on the box. "Keep my distance, and I'm locked in the basement like some family secret. Can I eat now?"

Jamilah stepped forward to open the box and handed Myra the dishes of food she had prepared for her, but Hassan grabbed her by the elbow.

"Remember my conditions, Jamilah."

Myra looked at Jamilah. "He's really serious about this ten feet thing, huh?"

"I am afraid so," Jamilah said, evidently embarrassed by Hassan's overprotectiveness.

Myra sat on the floor cross-legged and opened the lid of the box and tore into the food.

"In the name of Allah," Jamilah said. "We always say in the name of Allah before we eat."

Myra continued chewing the succulent lamb off the bone as if she didn't hear her. Jamilah and Hassan looked on in amazement as Myra devoured the plates of food as if they were appetizers.

"Do you have any more painkillers?" Myra asked Jamilah. "My ribs are throbbing."

Hassan withdrew the bottle of painkillers from his pocket and tossed them to Myra.

She popped two and chased them down with a pitcher of water. "What's in the bag?" she asked Hassan.

He untied it from his shoulder and lobbed it to her. The bag contained new underwear, two pair of cotton pants, and a few bars of soap.

"There's a bathroom and shower upstairs," Jamilah said. "Hassan will stand right outside the door while you shower." Jamilah looked at Myra seriously. "I hope I am not making a mistake by trusting you."

Myra stood up and swung the bag over her shoulder. "I'll keep my word; make sure you do the same. If you don't mind, I would like to take a shower before we get started."

"Yes, of course," Jamilah said. "You know my name, you know Hassan's name. What is your name?"

Myra thought about it for a moment and then said with a smirk. "Call me... Thalatha." That was the Arabic word for the number three.

Six months later, Jamilah surprised Myra with the speed at which she learned English. She even learned how to conceal her Arabic accent. Hassan had a couple surprises of his own. He had eased up on the ten feet rule. He still made Jamilah keep her distance, but he no longer tensed up when Jamilah would greet Myra every afternoon with a hug and the Muslim greeting (peace be upon you). He even started to smile. Especially when he would see the excitement on Jamilah's face after she correctly read an English sentence or paragraph that Myra had written on the cracked chalkboard.

Tonight, Myra was in the middle of doing her pushups when she heard the basement door being unlocked. She quickly stood up and cut out the light and hid behind a desk.

"Three, it's me," Hassan whispered, as he descended the steps and cut on the light.

Myra stood up from behind the desk. She could see the hurt in his face "What's wrong?"

"Jamilah respects you a lot. She praises your strength; you are like no woman she has ever seen."

Myra folded her arms and continued listening.

"Zakawi has broken many men, who were much stronger than you, in a matter of days. And if not days, it wouldn't take more than a week. You lasted nine months. Two weeks after you being captured, Zakawi no longer cared about what information you may have had. Your intolerance to his interrogation forced him to keep you alive. He knew that he had to break you before killing you. If not, he would lose face in the eyes of his men. I finally convinced him that it would be better to lie to the men, tell them that he broke you and to leave you in the desert for the dogs."

And why would you do that?"

"Because like Jamilah, I have come to respect you, as well."

Myra didn't react to the compliment. She needed to know where this conversation was going.

"But I didn't come here tonight to shower you with praises," Hassan said.

"I didn't think you did." Myra waited patiently as Hassan tried to force the words out of his moth. Myra cocked her head when she saw tears forming in the corner of his eyes.

"Zakawi…" Hassan finally said. "He has sent her away."

Myra's eyes widened. "Why would he do that?"

"He's planning something. Something big."

"I would ask you what, but I'm certain you wouldn't tell me."

"No, I wouldn't."

Myra looked at him suspiciously. "I've kept my word to Jamilah. So, are you here to keep her end of the bargain or… are you here to kill me?"

"I am here to honor Jamilah's word. You need to come with me now."

"Okay, I'm ready." Hassan turned to leave, Myra withdrew the ten-inch lead pipe she had concealed up her sleeve. "Hassan!" He turned right into the skull-crushing blow.

Hassan started coming around ten minutes later. He felt someone standing him up. Then he felt something being placed around his neck.

"Hey." Myra smacked him.

His eyes popped open and then sagged shut. Myra smacked him again. He tried to swing at her. That's when he realized his hands were bound behind his back. He tried to kick at her. That's when he realized his feet were bound. He saw a lamp cord tied onto the overhead beam directly above him. That's when he realized there was a noose around his neck.

"I will kill you for this," he said, and then spat in Myra's face.

Myra casually wiped off the spit and then struck him in the balls with the pipe. His knees buckled. The noose tightened around his neck, forcing him to stand back up and endure the pain ringing through his scrotum.

Myra flashed the knife she took from him while he was unconscious. Hassan's hunting knife was razor sharp. Myra had tasted its bite many times.

"I would love nothing more than to pay you back for the pain you inflicted upon me all these years," Myra said.

"I only did what I was ordered to do."

"Now, you're going to do what I order you to do. Tell me what Zakawi's planning?"

Hassan studied the knife in Myra's hand. "Kill me, because I will never tell you."

Myra followed his eyes to the knife and then chuckled. "The knife's not for you, Romeo. I just want you to look at it one last time. I'm going to find Jamilah. And when I do, I will use *this* knife to sever her fingers, one by one."

"You will never find her."

"Funny. Everyone said the same thing about me finding Zakawi."

Hassan's eyes widened.

"After severing her fingers, I will work my way up to her hands, then to her elbows. Then her shoulders."

"You demon!" Hassan shouted as he struggled to free his hands.

"I will cauterize her wounds so she will not die, but her dreams of practicing medicine will."

Hassan started cursing Myra.

Myra smirked. "Personally, I think she won't be able to live the rest of her life as a limbless cripple. It will only be a matter of time before she ends her life."

Hassan started to cry.

"Suicide is forbidden in Islam. Anyone who commits suicide will be in the hell-fire forever. Now tell me what Zakawi's planning!"

"How can you be so evil? She pleaded for your life, she's the reason you're still alive."

"I'll make sure I thank her, right before I help her slit her throat."

"May Allah curse you for all eternity."

"Good-bye, Hassan." Myra started heading up the stairs.

"Wait!" Hassan cried out.

"I'm listening."

"Zakawi's going to America."

"He's planning a terrorist attack on U.S. soil?"

Hassan nodded.

"What's the target?"

"I don't know. I swear by Allah, I don't know. I am to stay behind so I don't have any information on the attack."

"How many men is he taking?"

"None. The men and women are already in place."

"When is the attack taking place?"

"I don't know."

"I don't believe you."

"Why do you care? Your government left you to die, they even refused to acknowledge you even existed."

Myra started walking up the steps again.

"Wait! I overheard a name. It was American."

"What's the name?"

"Will you release me?"

"I will send someone to release you."

"Give me your word that you won't harm Jamilah, and that you will send someone for me."

"Even if I gave you my word, why would you believe it?"

"As evil as you are, you have honor."

Myra threw the knife at him. It sunk into the wooden chair near him. "If you're not lying to me, I give you my word, I won't go after Jamilah and you will not die down here."

Hassan nodded and with his heavy Arabic accent, he struggled to pronounce the American's name. "Victor's Papa."

The name didn't mean anything to Myra; at least not yet.

Thirteen hours later, Hassan's knees were seconds away from buckling for good. Myra had lied to him. She sent no one, and now he was going to die. He prayed to Allah. He prayed to Allah just as his knees gave. "Allah forgive me." His knees buckled for the last time. The noose bit into his neck.

He didn't fight the overwhelming sensation to stand back up, because he knew he couldn't prevent the inevitable. Just as he was about to pass out, something hit him on the side of the face. It was the floor. He lay on his side as he sucked air into his lungs. He finally managed to work his way over to the wooden chair and pulled out the knife with his teeth. He dropped it to the floor and grabbed it with his hands and cut the cords around his hands and feet.

He took the noose from around his neck and inspected it. Just as he thought, he could see where Myra had sliced it just enough to give way when it was forced to support his body weight. The demon had kept her word—he wouldn't die down there. He thought about going after Myra, but with a thirteen-hour head start, he knew she was long gone.

CHAPTER 10

*T*he present....

The soldier pulled up to Laura's apartment building. He got out and opened the car door for her. "Would you like me to escort you upstairs?"

"If it's not too much trouble," Laura said, looking up at her building.

As they headed into the apartment complex, Laura looked up and down the street. No one was in sight, and no one was sitting idle in any of the parked cars. The soldier walked in front of Laura, back straight, shoulders squared, like he was ready for combat. After what Laura saw tonight, Myra, Cleary, or Walker could take him out without breaking a sweat.

In the lobby, Laura tried to look around corners before they took them, and she waited for the soldier to step into the elevator before she entered, and she didn't get off the elevator until he walked out into the corridor and told her it was clear.

"Would you like me to do a walk-through the apartment?" he asked.

"Please do." Laura followed behind him as he checked every room and closet. He even checked the terrace and under the bed. They ended back in the living room.

"You're good to go," the soldier said. "You're on the thirteenth floor, so you don't have to worry about anyone coming through the terrace or windows." He cracked the front door. "Just keep your door locked, and you'll be—"

Myra put her whole body into the kick she delivered to the front door. The door crashed into the soldier's shoulder, knocking him back and off balance. Myra leaped forward, fist drawn back to her ear. The stunned soldier put his hands up to protect his face. Myra launched her punch to his solar plexus. The soldier lost all of his wind. As he doubled over, he tried engulfing Myra into a bear hug. She backpedaled. The soldier's arms wrapped around each other. Myra sprung right back at him with a front kick to his forehead, sending him flipping over the couch. His head bounced off the coffee table. Myra could tell he was out cold by the awkward angle his body laid.

Laura had been paralyzed the whole time. She still didn't move as Myra turned her attention to her. Myra hopped over the couch and crouched beside the soldier. She unsnapped the soldier's holster and took his 9mm and the two extra clips from his ammo pouch.

"You just going to stand there looking like a zombie?" Myra said to Laura. "Have a seat."

"Myra—

"I said have a seat." Myra pointed the gun at her. When Laura sat, Myra found the soldier's handcuffs and cuffed his hands behind his back. She looked down at him with disdain. "Newbies."

Laura sat in the armchair, shaking.

"You betrayed me, Doc."

"Myra—"

"Shut up!" Myra pointed the gun at her again. "Just shut up." Myra closed the front door and locked it, all the while, keeping the gun pointed at Laura. "I took a chance and trusted you, and look where it got me?"

"Major Jennings had my phone tapped, he heard everything. As far as Cleary goes, he must've just been following me around, hoping that you would try and make contact with me."

"The Major tapping your phone, Cleary following you, that all sounds real convenient."

"It's the truth."

"Ha!" Myra chuckled as she walked up on her. "If I believed everyone who told me that they were telling the truth, I would've been dead a long time ago."

"You *have* to believe me," Laura whispered.

Myra pressed the gun to Laura's head. "You don't tell me what I *have* to do."

"You're right," Laura said quickly. "I'm sorry."

"Now you're sorry?"

"I'm really sorry."

"If you say you're sorry one more time…" Myra pressed the gun harder against Laura's head.

Laura tried to shrink into the chair. Myra backed away from her and sat on the couch. She placed the gun in her lap and pulled out a bag of dope.

"My life is over, Doc." Myra tapped some of the heroin onto the back of her hand and sniffed it. "Don't act like you didn't know I was getting high. You're a psychiatrist; you're supposed to be able to detect shit like this. You knew, didn't you?"

"I didn't know until Major Jennings told me about the drugs and needles the cops found in your apartment."

Myra studied her for a moment. "Liar!" Myra snatched the gun off her lap and jumped up and took aim at Laura's head.

"Please, Myra, don't kill me." She started to cry.

Myra paced back and forth.

"You can still get out of this, Myra. No jury is going to convict you if—"

"A jury?" Myra said, not believing that Laura was that naïve. "Doc, I'll never see the inside of a court room. Did it look like Cleary was trying to take me in or take me out?"

"Major Jennings—" Laura started to say.

"Major Jennings." Myra started laughing. Myra's cut her laugh short and turned her attention to the house phone when it began ringing.

Laura shot out the chair and tackled Myra. Myra was in too shocked to feel the pain in her back when she hit the floor and Laura landed on top of her. Laura tried to wrench the gun out of Myra's hand.

Myra punched Laura in the face with her free hand. The blow stunned Laura long enough for Myra to flip her off her, but Laura didn't loosen her grip on the gun. Both women got to their feet, swinging at each other with their free hand. Myra ducked under Laura's last punch and drove her shoulder into Laura's stomach. The hit took all the air and fight out of Laura.

Myra slammed her against the wall and stabbed the gun into Laura's cheek. "Bye, Doc."

The phone's answering machine beeped to take a message. "Demon!"

Myra looked at the phone, eyes wide.

"Demon, I know you hear me. Remove the gun from the doctor's face and pick up the phone." His Arabic was crisp. Myra's body began to tremble on its own. "Demonnn. Pick. Up. The phone."

Myra lowered the gun and walked to the phone as if she was in a trance. She lifted the receiver to her ear.

"It seems like you have a problem staying dead," Zakawi said.

"Where are you?" Myra asked.

"A block away, watching you through the scope of a rifle."

Myra flipped off the light switch and ducked into the hallway, out of sight of all windows. But she made sure to keep Laura in gun sight.

"If I wanted to put a bullet in your head, I would've done it when you were sitting on the couch snorting your dope. I think it's time we meet face-to-face. I have a proposition for you."

"You know where I'm at," Myra said. "Come on over."

Zakawi laughed. "Still sarcastic and defiant as ever, I see."

"So what's the Doc supposed to be? Part of your international harem?"

"She was a means to an end. And now that I have what I want, she's of no use to me."

"So, I can put a bullet in her brain?"

"That would save me the trouble of having to do it."

"Fuck you!"

"Now, now, demon. Is that anyway to talk to your fellow terrorist?"

"There's only one terrorist on this line."

"I find that hard to believe," Zakawi chuckled. "You were just weeks away from helping a deep-cover Iraqi cell blow up the United Nations building."

Myra was silent.

"You're good," Zakawi said. "How you were able to locate the cell and get them to let you play a key role in the bombing was sheer genius. You should've seen the look on my face when Ashraf showed me a photo of the American who was going to help him and his cell bring down America. He said it was as if I'd seen a ghost."

"I have that effect on people," Myra said sarcastically.

"My first impulse was to send a team to your apartment and eliminate you, but then I thought, could the demon who used to talk in her sleep about killing those who abandoned her really go through with it, or was she just babbling? I didn't think you had the balls."

"I bet you'd like to see them, so you could see what a real pair looks like."

"Is that an invite?" Zakawi asked.

"To meet face-to-face or for you to suck my balls?"

"Demon you really try my patience with your sarcasm. You are like a deeply embedded splinter. Too deep to see, but the pain lets me know that it's still there."

"That's the nicest thing anyone has ever said about me."

"Let's meet Demon, face-to-face."

"Can't," Myra said.

"Why not?"

"Because there's a 99 percent chance that I will kill you on sight."

Zakawi laughed. "In my business, those are pretty good odds. Meet with me, Specialist Myra Taft, U.S. Army. I promise you won't be disappointed."

"Give me one good reason why I should."

"The enemy of my enemy…"

"Is my friend," Myra said, finishing off the quote. There was a gut-wrenching silence before Myra answered. "When and where?"

"I'll call you tomorrow with an address and time. Until then, try and stay alive."

"As you witnessed, I do that very well."

Zakawi laughed and ended the call. Myra turned the lights back on and walked up on Laura. Without warning, she slapped her. The slap nearly knocked Laura out. She staggered sideways and used her hands to break her fall. She landed on her side and hurried up and covered her face, waiting for a barrage of blows that never came. She peeked over her hands and saw Myra just standing over her shaking her head.

"How long have you been keeping tabs on me for Zakawi?"

"In my bedroom," Laura said, "there's a DVD, it will explain everything."

Myra allowed her to stand up. Myra followed her to the bedroom and watched her slide a DVD into the player. Someone was holding a camcorder to the ground. As the person slowly raised it, Myra stopped breathing. She would never forget the cave she was in for months. The scene was the same, the only difference was she wasn't the one stretched across the rock slab. A man was. A man in a shredded Army uniform. He was unchained and helped into a sitting position. The person working the camcorder zoomed in on the soldier's bloodied and bruised face. Laura began to sob.

The soldier was handed a piece of paper to read from. He looked down at it, barely able to see it through his blackened and swollen eyes.

"Laura, I'm being held by a militia. Our convoy was ambushed; I'm the only survivor." The soldier started crying. "Laura, I don't want to die."

Laura fell to her knees and broke into tears.

The soldier continued. "They said that if you don't do exactly as I say, they will... they will torture and then kill me. They will film it and send it to you." The soldier couldn't continue reading; he was crying too hard. Myra heard someone shouting in Arabic for the soldier to keep reading. A hand shot out from behind the camcorder and struck the soldier in the face. Blood started to flow from the soldier's nose.

"Laura, please do *exactly* what the woman tells you to do. Once you help her complete her mission, they will release me. They've given me their word and I believe them."

The screen went black. Myra looked down at Laura, who looked like she was a breath away from a nervous breakdown. Myra kneeled down beside her.

"Who's the kid?" Myra asked.

Laura took a deep breath. "He's my little brother." Laura hugged Myra and started crying even harder. Myra stiffened, not knowing if she should hug her or push her away. Myra slowly brought her hands up and wrapped them around Laura. Myra tightened her embrace around her as her dam of tears broke, as well. Seeing the cave she'd been in, knowing the pain those bastards were inflicting on Laura's brother, who didn't look a day over twenty, shattered her super soldier persona. If Zakawi had any idea what was running through Myra's mind, right now, he would do himself a favor and put a gun to his head and pull the trigger.

"Tell me about the woman," Myra said.

"I got the DVD in the mail with a letter that ordered me to view the DVD and then wait to be contacted. The letter also said that if I alerted anyone, the threat against my brother would immediately be carried out. The next morning she walked into my office and told me what she wanted me to do."

"And what was that?"

Laura kept her head down. "Tape our sessions and then give them to her."

"What else?" Myra asked.

"That's all I was instructed to do until the incident at your apartment."

"What did she want you to do after the incident at my apartment?"

Laura unbuttoned her shirt, exposing the wireless mic clipped to her bra. She saw the question mark in Myra's eyes and answered it before she had a chance to ask it. "It's not on. I was only instructed to activate it when the police or someone from the Army came to see me. Or if you ever made contact with me."

"I'm making contact with you now."

"You kinda caught me off guard with the way you steam-rolled in here kicking ass, snorting dope, and waving a gun around."

"Describe the woman."

"You met with her in a diner."

Myra cocked her head.

"Major Jennings showed me some pictures of people who you were meeting with around town. He asked me if any of them looked familiar."

"What did you tell him?"

"I told him I didn't recognize any of them, but he said he was going to round them up and detain them for questioning.

Myra nodded slowly. That explained why Zakawi wanted to meet. If Jennings rounded up the members of the cell, Zakawi would have to alter his plan. Myra was back in the game. Myra headed into the living room with Laura hot on her heels. Myra checked on the soldier to make sure he was still unconscious. "I have to go, Doc."

"Go? Why?"

The soldier's cell phone rang.

"That's why," Myra said. "A few seconds later, Laura's house phone rang. "It's Jennings. He's wondering why his man hasn't checked in yet."

"I'll tell him that—"

Myra held her hand up. "There's nothing to tell. Jennings already dispatched a team when soldier boy here didn't check in."

"How do you know tha—" Before Laura could finish her thought, Myra had leaped over the couch and braced herself against the wall behind the front door. A fraction of a second later, Cleary kicked open the door. Myra didn't miss a beat; she kicked it right back at him. He wasn't expecting the door to come rushing right back at him. It slammed into his extended forearms, knocking his gun from his hand. Myra flung the door open while firing at the same time. Cleary and Walker had already removed themselves from the doorway. Myra still had the advantage of catching them off guard. With the hammerless .38 in one hand, and the soldier's 9mm in the other, she ran into the corridor, arms extended, firing blindly down both sides of the hallway. Cleary and Walker had ducked into the stairwell just as three bullets whizzed by their heads.

Myra hit the elevator's call button with the butt of her gun while keeping her eye and 9mm trained on the stairwell.

"Taft!" Cleary called out. "When I get my hands on you—"

"Blow me." Myra entered the elevator and hit the lobby button. When the doors closed, she kept her eyes on the numbers as they lit up in descending order. Myra knew Walker would remain on Laura's floor to track the elevator's steady descent, while Cleary flew down the stairwell to catch up with the elevator. It's what she would do. That slice of information was her only advantage. If Cleary just concentrated on flying down the thirteen flights of steps, he would surely beat the elevator to the lobby, but Myra knew he wouldn't just head for the lobby; he had learned to always expect the unexpected from Demon Three.

But what if she was wrong? What if he was heading straight for the lobby? Myra stopped breathing as the elevator stopped on the third floor. Shit, she thought. What if he got to the third floor ahead of the elevator and hit the call button? Myra pictured him in a gun shooter's stance, waiting for the doors to open. She turned her body sideways trying to make herself as small a target as possible. She held her left arm straight out while bending her right at the elbow. She looked like she was drawing the string on a bow and arrow. Both guns were sighted where she thought Cleary's head would be when the doors opened. As the doors began to part, Myra looped her index fingers around the trigger of each gun and exhaled.

A white-haired woman who was waiting on the elevator stared at Myra as if she was the Angel of Death who had come to claim her soul. The woman clutched her chest and fainted. Myra dashed out of the elevator and ran for the stairwell. She shouldered the door and listened. She could hear Cleary barreling down the steps. It sounded as if he was only two flights away. Myra took off down the stairs.

Myra stuffed the guns in her vest pockets as she hit the lobby. She flew out the building, heading for Soldier boy's SUV. Myra ducked as a bullet shattered the passenger side window. Cleary's next two shots flattened the passenger side tires.

"Fuck!" Myra peeped over the hood and saw Cleary running toward the SUV, firing his gun. She pulled out the hammerless .38 and fired blindly over the hood until it was empty. Once empty, she tossed it and pulled out Soldier boy's 9mm. Cleary had ducked behind a car. She knew Walker was on his way down, and together they would surely annihilate her. She fired two rounds into the car Cleary took cover behind and took off running.

Myra heard hooting and hollering from the three hard-looking thugs who had witnessed the gunplay between her and Cleary. Myra ducked and zigzagged as bullets hit the ground on either side of her.

The next one's a head shot," Cleary yelled.

Myra stopped running and turned around. Cleary was walking toward her, gun pointed at her.

"Drop the gun," Cleary said to Myra.

She judged the distance between her and Cleary. He was about fifty feet away and closing fast. Myra was a better shot than him, but by the time she raised her gun and pulled the trigger, he would have pulled his trigger three to four times. She dropped her gun and held her hands up shoulder-level, palms facing Cleary.

"Didn't think you were going to take me in alive," Myra shouted.

Cleary smirked. "Who said anything about taking you in alive?"

Cleary and Myra flinched and ducked when they heard the gunshots. The three hard-looking thugs had pulled out guns and were shooting at Cleary. He fired back as their bullets forced him to take cover.

Myra scooped up her gun and took off running.

"Myra!" Cleary called out." He gritted his teeth when he saw her cut the corner. She was going to get away once again.

Walker bolted out of the apartment building, his hand already pulling the Uzi from under his jacket. The Uzi looked like it was spitting fire when he let off a barrage of bullets at the thugs. The thugs jumped, crawled, and rolled over each other, trying to duck behind the row of parked cars.

Cleary popped up from his shelter and dashed to the car and started it up. Walker jumped in, while keeping his gun trained at the row of cars the thugs dashed behind.

As Cleary skidded around the corner, Walker hit the dashboard and pointed. "There she is."

Myra heard the screeching tires and ran faster. Twenty yards away she saw it. A guy on a Yamaha, helmet in hand, pimp smile on his face, as he tried laying his mack down on the girl he had rolled up on. Still running at top speed, Myra aimed the 9mm at Playboy's helmet and squeezed off a shot.

"Oh, shit!" Playboy yelled as he dropped his helmet as if it was on fire. Him and his bike fell over.

"Fuck out the way," Myra said, as she ran up on him. He scuttled away from the bike, holding his hands in the air. The girl stared in shock as Myra picked up the bike and revved it. "What are you looking at?" Myra asked the girl and then snatched the shades off the girl's face. Myra slipped them on and peeled off.

Myra looked in the rearview mirror. Cleary was gaining on her. She kicked the bike up two gears and leaned the top half of her body against the bike's gas tank as she opened the throttle all the way. The bike jerked forward as it easily hit sixty. Myra had green lights for six blocks.

On the seventh, the light turned yellow. On the eighth, it was red. She downshifted as she approached the boulevard and hit the rear brakes and leaned into the turn. The bike fishtailed and got so low that Myra's knee nearly touched the ground. When she hit the boulevard corner, she popped the clutch and gunned the throttle. The bike straightened up and shot forward.

Cleary took the corner without slowing. His car fishtailed into the string of garbage cans lining the curb, sending them catapulting through the air like missiles.

Myra took the next corner, putting a little more distance between her and Cleary. She dipped into an alley and swerved around the debris while Cleary smashed through it all. Myra shot out the other end and leaned into the right turn.

Her eyes widened behind the shades as she saw the traffic up ahead. She hopped the bike onto the sidewalk and beeped the horn as she tried her best to dodge the people in her way. One was too slow getting out of the way and she clipped him, sending him twisting through the air. She hopped back onto the street when she got ahead of the traffic. She heard a loud crash and looked back. Cleary had slammed his way through the traffic jam.

Myra knew she had to end this, and quick, before the police picked up the chase. She hit the front brake. While holding the front brake down, Myra opened the throttle, causing the bike to do a one-eighty turn. She popped the clutch and set the bike on a head-on collision with Cleary.

Cleary tightened his grip on the steering wheel and put the pedal to the floor.

Myra pulled out the nine and fired at Cleary's side of the windshield. He gritted his teeth and ducked as the bullets penetrated the windshield, but he kept the car on a collision course with Myra. Walker grinned and braced himself for the collision.

Myra lowered the gun two inches and fired.

"No," Cleary and Walker both said, as they realized what Myra's intentions were from the get go. She emptied the rest of the clip into the car's grill. Cleary began to yank the steering wheel to the left, but it was too late. Not too many people knew that firing bullets into the grill of a car triggers the airbags. Cleary lost control of the car as the airbags exploded into their faces. The car crashed into the back of a delivery truck.

Myra zoomed past them. She looked in her rearview and saw when Cleary opened the car and crawled out. She tucked the nine back in her vest and headed for the highway. She looked down at her vest pocket when Laura's phone started to vibrate. She ignored it until she reached the highway then finally answered it.

"Well done, demon," Zakawi said.

"Time and place," Myra said.

"Patience, Demon."

"Patience my ass. Time is running out for me."

Zakawi remained silent.

"Time, place, or fuck off!"

"I will call you tomorrow night at ten o' clock with an address. Don't disappoint me, demon. Until then, I'm quite sure you'll find something to do."

Myra ended the call and unclipped the spare helmet off the bike and pulled it on. *Yeah,* Myra thought, *I do have something to do.*

CHAPTER 11

*M*ajor Jennings sat in the back of a burgundy SUV, cell still in his hand, eyes closed. He just got off the phone with the two soldiers he sent to Laura's apartment. The Demons had turned East New York into a war zone. He was able to keep the shootout at the abandoned chicken spot under wraps, but this... He opened his eyes and looked down at his phone as it vibrated in his hand. The caller ID read Blocked. Jennings sighed.

"Jennings," He said when he answered it.

"What the hell are you doing?"

Jennings sat up and pressed the phone harder to his ear. "Sir, I was planning on calling you first thing in the morning to explain—"

"Explain now. I gave you a direct order to stay out of the way of my demons."

"I know, but I thought—"

"You thought? You don't get paid to think, you get paid to follow orders."

"Yes, sir."

"Do I have to repeat my orders?"

"No, sir."

"And Major, if you in anyway interfere with my demons again, I'll personally see to it that you lose everything."

Jennings felt his blood pressure rise when the Director of Special Operations ended the call. The Director had only spoken directly to Jennings on two occasions. The first time was at the Pentagon when Myra's team was being put together. And the second was tonight. The Director talked to no one directly, except the Secretary of Defense or the President of the United States. So tonight's phone call was more than the Director reiterating his orders; it was a warning. "Lose everything" could mean anything from having his pension snatched to "slipping" in the shower and breaking his neck.

Jennings entered his home and went through his ritual of tossing his keys on the hallway table and then fixing himself a drink in his den. He poured himself two fingers of vodka and tossed it back. He grabbed the bottle and sat at his desk. He poured himself another shot and tossed it back. He squinted at the corner of the room where the darkness seemed to come alive.

Myra split the darkness, gently tapping her gun against her thigh. "What's up, Major?"

Jennings grabbed the bottle and slowly poured himself another drink and gulped it. In his nervousness, the vodka went down the wrong pipe. He started coughing. During his coughing fit, Jennings subtly began reaching for the handgun he had mounted under his desk.

Myra raised her gun and aimed at his chest. Jennings recognized the gun immediately.

"Looking for this?" Myra asked.

Jennings's eyes started to water. "Myra—"

"Why, old man?"

"Why what?" Jennings said unconvincingly.

"Good bye, old man." Myra's finger tensed on the trigger.

Jennings laughed a nervous laugh. "You have no idea what's going on. If I answered your question, you'll be more confused than you are now."

Myra's facial expression didn't change. She was going to shoot him.

"God dammit, Myra. This is how you're going to treat me? After all I've done for you?"

"I love you, old man, which is why this hurts so much." Myra's hand started to shake. She sniffled and blinked away the tears forming on the edges of her eyes. "I don't give a fuck that you betrayed your country, but to betray me... why me?"

Jennings gnawed on his lip as he stared down the barrel of the gun. "Your unit's nothing new. I came up with the idea of infiltrating terrorist cells and destroying them from the inside out in the 80's. It was *my* program, and *I* had the perfect candidate. Arab-born, so he didn't have to learn the language or the customs. Lived in Iran and Iraq all his life so I didn't have to create a false history for him. He had already established himself as an arms dealer during the Iran-Contra era. His loyalty to Saddam's cause was unquestionable when he fought against us in Desert Storm. We trained him. We transformed him from a common guerilla soldier to the perfect weapon."

"Zakawi." Myra whispered.

Jennings nodded.

"Seems like your perfect weapon didn't turn out to be so perfect, huh?"

"When he agreed to work for me, he had one stipulation—he would help us win the war on Terror as long as we gave our word that we would never invade his homeland."

"Iraq," Myra said.

"Fucking Peter Folks. You would swear he's the Secretary of Defense with the way the President listens to him."

"What *is* the Secretary of Defense saying about this?"

Jennings averted his gaze.

Myra cocked her head. "You've got to be shitting me. He doesn't know. What about Folks?"

"Zakawi was *my* special op."

"But you don't run Special Ops anymore. You had an obligation to brief your successor on all operations, past and ongoing, but you didn't. You left Zakawi out... purposely." Myra just connected the last dot.

Major Jennings knew she had by the look on her face. "I'm seventy-two years old, fifty-one of those, I've spent risking my life for this country. And what thanks do I get? I get *my program* snatched from me and given to a snot-nosed kid who was in diapers when I was running covert operations all over the world. Fifty-one years. Look at me. I've been reduced to an Army psychiatrist with an office no bigger than a cubicle, and my pension is smaller than that."

"So, this is about money."

"This is about revenge!" The veins in Jennings neck bulged. "This country betrayed me and they betrayed you. I didn't betray you, I didn't leave you to the mercy of those savages for three years."

"Don't—" Myra said through her bared teeth. Jennings jerked back in his chair as Myra cocked the hammer on the nine. "You can just miss me with that psycho-babble bullshit."

"Myra, put the gun down; together we can make sure Myra Taft, the murderer/cop shooter dies. The police will corner her off in the basement of an abandoned building. Ten minutes later, the basement will explode in a big ball of fire. Myra Taft will be blown to pieces. We're all on the same side; you, me, Zakawi. I know about the bombing that's supposed to take place at the U.N." Myra's look of shock gave Jennings a little confidence.

"Yes, I know all about it, but what *you* don't know is that's not the intended target. Ashraf and his team were just a distraction, suicide mission. Don't you see what I did? I rounded them up so that Zakawi would have no choice but to make contact with you."

Myra put her head down.

"Zakawi contacted you hasn't he?"

Myra didn't answer.

Jennings took that as a yes. "Don't you see? Zakawi may not work for me anymore, directly, but I still have my ways of controlling him. By rounding up his key players, I left him with no choice but to contact you. He won't cancel or postpone his attack, because he's waited too long. You, me, and Zakawi may not see eye-to-eye, but we want the same thing. I've put you in a position to be part of the real mission."

"And what is the real mission?"

"Not what, who." Jennings looked over his shoulder at the portrait hanging on the wall. "I have a safe behind the picture. In it is a folder that will explain everything." He got to his feet and removed the portrait so Myra could see the safe.

Myra slowly lowered her gun as he began punching in the numbers. She

broke out into a sweat. She needed to snort a couple lines. Everything was making sense. Zakawi an U.S. trained guerilla, Jennings a disgruntled war horse forced into shuffling papers behind a desk, and of course an Army-trained counter-terrorist, ex prisoner of war, dope fiend junkie. They were the *perfect* band to topple America or hand it over to...

Both Myra and Jennings froze. The buzzing of busy insects came to a halt and was replaced by the flapping wings of birds abruptly leaving their nests. Two telltale signs a seasoned warrior recognized before a firefight.

Myra reacted without thinking twice. She dove to the ground a split second before the bullets tore through the den's window. Jennings, whose reflexes had been dulled by years of sitting behind a desk, didn't think of diving for cover until a bullet ricocheted off the safe door and grazed his hand. As he dove to the ground, a bullet pierced his right calve. He crumpled to the ground.

"No!" Myra watched as Jennings hit the floor face first. She watched helplessly as Jennings forced himself to crawl to the paper shredder next to his desk and feed the folder into it. He smiled weakly and collapsed with a thud.

Fuck! Myra crawled out of the den and into the living room on her elbows and knees. Round after round of bullets turned the living room into a battlefield of shattered glass, splintered wood, and puffs of feathers from the living room furniture.

Myra crawled under the grand piano and calmed her mind as she focused on an escape route. The dust from the sheet-rocked living room wall allowed her to see the infrared beams from the snipers's rifles crisscrossing the living room, lingering long enough on each piece of furniture until the sniper was satisfied that she wasn't behind it. Myra quickly ran through the list of probable shooters. Definitely wasn't the demons; too much noise and too many bullets. Wasn't Army; they wouldn't have dared open fire with Jennings in the room. The Police force? No, they would've had a negotiator on the bullhorn by now. Zakawi? Maybe. Whoever it was, had her pinned. There was no way she could get to the back or front door without presenting herself as a target for the snipers. Myra huffed. She had two options. Wait to see if they come in for her, or a nosy neighbor called the police.

Myra cocked her head when she heard the knob of the front door turn. The door was locked so it wouldn't be that easy for whoever it was to come in. Myra tightened her finger on the trigger and closed her eyes. She found that closing her eyes heightened her sense of hearing. Myra didn't flinch when the door was kicked off its hinges. She took a deep breath and waited for the assailant to step inside the house. No need in shooting blindly. Right now, every bullet counted.

"Peace be upon you," a female's voice said from the front door. "Three, are you there?"

Myra opened her eyes. She recognized the voice immediately. "Jamilah?"

Myra stood up from behind the piano. Jamilah looked far from the eighteen year old she remembered. Jamilah replaced her modest dress for a pair of jeans and leather jacket. Her head wasn't covered. Jamilah's hair was pulled back into a ponytail. What surprised Myra the most was the hardness of Jamilah's face. She was no longer the innocent little girl who thought that all of the world's leaders would one day hold hands and sing *We are the World.*

Myra caught the movement in her peripheral but it was too late. One of Jamilah's men snuck up on Myra while she was taking a trip down memory lane. Myra tried to duck the butt of the man's rifle, but it had already found its mark. Myra glanced at Jamilah before she blacked out and cursed herself for trusting her. After all, she was the daughter of America's most wanted terrorist.

CHAPTER 12

M yra was jolted awake by a prodding hand against her head. She blinked a couple of faces into focus. None of which looked familiar, but the off-the-rack-suits did.

"Sorry about your head," the one on the right said. He was a white male, muscular build, strong jaw. Definitely ex-Military. The other white male stood a couple feet back and watched the stare down between Myra and the man who whacked her over the head with the butt of his rifle.

"Name's Dan," the ex-Military guy said.

Myra looked around the room and realized that she was in a police station interrogation room, complete with a one-way mirror.

Dan winked at her. "You're special, sweetheart, the whole wing of this precinct has been reserved just for you. It's off limits to everyone. The Mayor himself can't even get in here."

Myra jerked both hands up until the cuffs that were fastened on either side of the chair stopped her from raising them any higher. "I'm not that special."

"Au contraire, darling. Not just anyone gets to wear *my* handcuffs. You have to be really special." Dan got right up in her face. "And you, dear, are really special."

Myra flinched, Dan jerked back, Myra laughed.

"Enough!" the second suit finally spoke. "I'm Special Agent Rutger, Homeland Security."

"Wow," Myra said. "And the plot thickens."

"You think this is a joke?" Dan opened his hand to smack Myra

"Dan!" Rutger called out to him.

Dan stopped in mid-swing, his face hell-red. Myra could tell he was biting down on his tongue to restrain his anger. Yeah, he was definitely ex-Military, and from his short fuse and buzz cut, he was definitely ex-Marine. Special Ops, no doubt.

"You know why you're here," Rutger said to Myra. "So, let's stop playing games. I want to know where Zakawi is, and I want the location of his supposed attack."

"Since when is it sanctioned to shoot a Major of the U.S. Army?" Myra asked.

"He's a fucking traitor to his country," Dan spat out.

Dan spoke of Jennings in the present tense, which meant he was alive, Myra noted.

"Zakawi," Rutger said, getting back to the question at hand. "Where is he and what's his target?"

"Ask his daughter," Myra said, cutting her eyes at the one-way mirror.

Rutger squinted his eyes at Myra and then left the interrogation room.

Dan eyed Myra. His facial gestures told her that he was an Alpha male; used to getting his way, short-tempered, and couldn't see past his ego. The flaring of the nose, upturning of the upper lip, and the gritting of the teeth also told her that he believed that women had no place in the armed forces. Myra added that mental note to the others. In a matter of minutes, she would formulate the perfect plan to make Dan her string less puppet.

Rutger returned a few minutes later with Jamilah. Myra couldn't take her eyes off her. Jamilah didn't make eye contact. Myra said something to her in Arabic. Jamilah responded in Arabic.

"English!" Dan said to Myra. "You are an American, or did they take that from you, too, after they broke you and made you their lap dog?"

"Take these handcuffs off and I'll show you who's the lap-dog." Dan chuckled, but his smile couldn't camouflage the rage in his eyes. "Just as I thought; another pussy Marine."

Dan rushed her.

"Dan," Rutger called out, but Dan had already kicked Myra in the chest, sending her and the chair she was cuffed to tumbling across the room. "I got your pussy." Dan nearly ripped off his front pocket as he dug for the handcuff key. Jamilah started screaming something in Arabic, Rutger ran across the room and jerked Dan away from Myra and snatched the cuff key from him.

"Get out of here, now" Rutger ordered Dan.

Dan looked at Rutger like he wanted to take his head off.

Rutger sensed it and stepped up into Dan's face. "I'm not going to say it again."

Dan palmed the top of his own head and rubbed it. He gave Myra one last stare before leaving the room. Jamilah ran to Myra and lifted the chair back into the upright position.

"Don't forget about what we discussed," Rutger said to Jamilah. He adjusted his tie and left the room, making sure to close the door behind himself.

"Get off me," Myra said to Jamilah in Arabic. "What kind of game are you playing?"

Jamilah twisted a strand of her hair and stared at the floor. "I…" Jamilah stammered as she struggled to find the right words to express herself. "The night I left Iraq wasn't planned. I wanted to come to you and tell you myself, but my father… he came home that night and told me he was sending me away, that he could no longer keep me safe. I pulled Hassan to the side and told him that he was to release you and assist you in getting back to your people. My father then whisked me away to the airport where I boarded a military plane."

"A military plane?"

Jamilah knew what Myra was really asking. "It was American. The military plane landed in Yemen. From there, I was given my papers and a student visa and then put on a civilian plane to America."

"Congratulations, on your dream coming true," Myra said.

"Yes, it did. I was attending Columbia University in New York City."

"Was?" Myra said picking up on the past tense.

"Last December, Special Agent Rutger came to my apartment with a team of officers and I was… I was arrested and placed into custody." Jamilah stopped twisting the lock of her hair and dabbed at her eyes to keep the tears from falling. "I committed no crime, but he told me that that didn't matter, that Homeland Security has the right to detain anyone, at any time, for how ever long they want."

"Good ole U.S of A," Myra chuckled. "So let me guess, they got wind that your father was in the country, and they want you to help them locate him. If you do, they'll let you go back to living your dream of becoming a doctor and working at a prestige American hospital. Hence, here you are trying to convince me that I should tell Dumb and Dumber out there where they might find your father?"

Jamiliah didn't respond.

"How could you turn on your father?" Myra asked with distain.

"What he is doing is wrong," Jamilah shouted. "What he is doing is not Islam."

"He's fighting the disbelievers who invaded his land. That *is* Islam," Myra countered.

"Don't." Jamilah pointed a trembling finger at Myra. "You know nothing of Islam. All you know is how to twist the truth."

Myra just stared at Jamilah and shook her head.

"Stop looking at me like that," Jamilah cried. "I'm doing the right thing."

Myra snorted. "We'll see who's right."

Both women looked toward the door when it swung open.

"I need to see you now," Rutger said to Jamilah.

"Sir—" Jamilah started to say.

Rutger walked up on her, grabbed her by the elbow and ushered her out of the room. When they entered the room adjacent from Myra, Rutger passed Jamilah off to Dan.

"You will do exactly what he tells you to do," Rutger said to Jamilah. "Am I clear?"

"Yes," Jamilah said, nodding obediently.

Rutger disappeared down the hall.

"What's going on?" Jamilah asked Dan.

"Nothing," Dan responded as he stared at Myra through the one-way mirror. "Just be ready to leave when I say so."

Rutger straightened his tie and smoothed back his hair as he approached the sergeant's desk at the front of the precinct. Sergeant Cleary looked beyond the Sergeant who was keeping him at bay at the desk and locked eyes with Rutger. Cleary reached into his inside pocket and pulled out a document.

"This is for her immediate release into my custody," Cleary said, holding the document toward Rutger.

"I'm special agent Rutger, " Rutger said, without bothering to take the document.

"I don't care who you are," Cleary said, as he unfolded the document and held it in Rutger's face so he could read it.

Rutger chewed on the inside of his cheek as he stared at the official seal at the bottom of the document and the unmistakable signature of The Director of Special Operations. Rutger took the document from Cleary and inspected it carefully and then nodded. "Okay... I just have to call my boss—"

"This is a release signed from your boss's boss," Cleary said, taking a step toward Rutger. "You don't want to fuck with me."

"You better back up… soldier," Rutger growled.

"Guys," the police sergeant said, as he got in between them. He then turned to Rutger and spoke, "Hurry up and call your boss so the both of you can get the hell out of my precinct."

Rutger pulled out his phone, while still keeping his eye on Cleary and hit speed dial. He turned his back on Cleary when Dan picked up. "Move 'em now."

"On my way out," Dan said. He then turned to Jamilah. "You stay right behind me, you understand?"

"What's going on?"

"I said do you understand?"

"Yes… I understand."

Dan busted into the interrogation room and uncuffed one of Myra's hands.

"You're releasing me?" Myra said.

"You wish."

He cuffed her free hand to her other hand then hoisted her to her feet. "Let's go."

"What's the rush?" Myra asked, seeing the sense of urgency in his face.

"Just shut up and do as you're told." He shoved her out of the room, and down the hall toward the back of the precinct. He looked over his shoulder to make sure Jamilah was still behind him. She was right on his heels. He shouldered the backdoor and pulled Myra out behind him toward an unmarked SUV.

"Hmm," Myra uttered, as she eyed the black and chrome H2 Hummer. "Homeland security is living it up."

Dan hit the button on his key ring, unlocking the Hummer and pushed Myra to the driver's backdoor. "Shut up and climb in." Once Myra was in, he cuffed her hands to the reinforced metal ring that was wielded on the back of the driver's seat.

"What's the hold up?" Cleary said to Rutger.

Rutger pretended to be talking to someone on the phone. He held a finger up to let Cleary know he was almost done.

Cleary fished his cellphone out his pocket as a text message came in from Walker. He read it and then looked at Rutger with a sinister grin that made him shudder.

What the fuck is he grinning about? Rutger said to himself. "Sorry, but I'm having trouble reaching my boss."

"I'm quite sure you have another number that you can try and reach him at, correct?"

"Actually, there is," Rutger said, opening his phone and dialing another number. This time he dialed his home number and listened to the answering machine. Rutger's eyes widened as he figured out what Andrew's sinister grin was all about. *He's fucking playing me.* Rutger hung up and called Dan's cell.

Cleary and Walker cased the precinct before Cleary went in. They already knew that there were only three exits out of the stationhouse. They also knew that if Homeland Security had to make a speedy escape, it would be the side or back exit. They both smiled at one another when they saw the black and chrome Hummer parked at the back of the police station. The Hummer was so Homeland Security.

Walker dropped Cleary at the front of the precinct and drove back around to the rear exit. Ten minutes after Cleary entered the precinct, a burly man with a buzz cut came flying out of the back entrance with Myra and Jamilah in tow. Walker texted Cleary, letting him know that Elvis had left the building. Their plan of separating the two agents and flushing their target out of the precinct had worked. Walker discretely followed the Hummer. In a few moments, he would have Myra in his possession, hopefully without having to kill the agent. Walker didn't have a problem killing. He just had a problem killing Americans, especially on U.S. soil, but as he knew just like his superiors that every war has its casualties.

Rutger kept his phone glued to his ear as it rang. *C'mon, Dan, pick up.* He looked up at Cleary as Dan's phone continued to ring. Cleary winked at him, solidifying the fact to Rutger that he had been played.

"What's up?" Dan said, as he answered his phone.

Rutger breathed a sigh of relief and spun so Cleary couldn't hear his conversation. "Dan, I think they're playing us. Are you being followed?"

"No."

"Are you sure?" Rutger said with urgency.

"I said no," Dan said, irritated that Rutger would question his counter-surveillance skills. "What do you mean by playing us?"

"I don't know; I just don't like the fact that this guy is acting... too cool."

"He's acting too cool?" Dan chuckled.

"Who's acting too cool?" Myra said from the backseat.

Dan looked in the rearview mirror. "Shut your mouth before I come back there and—" Dan saw the blue van from the opposite direction swerve into his lane. He hit the brakes on the Hummer, causing it to stop on a dime, but the forward momentum caused him to jerk forward. His cellphone slipped from between his ear and shoulder and dropped, bouncing off the steering wheel and then off his knee. Dan looked on open-eyed as the van fishtailed and the side door slid open. He saw the muzzle flashes before he heard the bullets pinging off the Hummer's grille and hood. He grabbed Jamilah and sought cover under the dashboard.

"Dan!" Rutger shouted into the phone. He spun, intending to grab Cleary by his throat and choking the life out of him, but when he spun around, Cleary was gone. "Where'd he go?" Rutger said to the police sergeant.

The sergeant shrugged. "He walked out the front door."

Rutger ran out of the police station and looked both ways, only to confirm what he already knew—Cleary was long gone.

"Keep your head down!" Dan yelled at Jamilah. He put the Hummer in reverse, and without raising his head from under the dashboard; he floored the gas pedal. The monstrous Hummer jerked as its wheels gripped the road and began picking up speed. Dan's heart started pounding in his chest because he was driving blind. He couldn't chance looking above the dashboard and catching a bullet between the eyes, but he also knew he couldn't just pray that they would keep going in reverse without hitting something. Dan knew once the Hummer stopped moving, they would be dead.

"Turn the wheel to the right," Myra barked from the backseat. Unlike Dan, Myra was used to bullets whizzing by her head. She looked through the rear windshield long enough to see the parked car they were heading for. "You're about to hit a parked car."

Without giving it a second thought, Dan spun the wheel to the right. The Hummer missed the parked car by inches. He took a chance and looked over the dashboard when he stopped hearing the pinging of bullets. The men had stopped firing on the Hummer and were getting back into the van. Dan watched as the van's back tires peeled off a long line of tire smoke as it headed straight for them. The van's tires weren't the only thing smoking. Smoke was coming from the Hummer's punctured radiator. The engine putted a couple times and then died.

"Fuck me," Dan yelled, as the Hummer coasted backwards. "This just can't get any worst."

A bullet whizzed by his ear.

"Ho, shit." He grabbed his ear and instinctively looked behind him in the direction the bullet came from. A man standing in front of his opened car door fired two more carefully placed shots. Both shots aimed directly at his head. Dan ducked and slammed on the brakes. He reached in his shoulder holster and pulled out his 9mm.

"Are you serious?" Myra said. She was looking at him from between the seats.

"Shut the fuck up!" Dan screamed. He nudged Jamilah's trembling arm off his shoulder. "You're doing good; just keep your head down."

Jamilah was too shaken up to respond.

Dan opened the glove compartment and pulled out another gun—a forty-five caliber.

Myra kicked the back of his seat. "Hand me one of those."

"Get the fuck out here," Dan yelled. "Just keep your head down and your mouth shut."

"You're getting gunfire from the front and back," Myra said. "Your vehicle has been disabled and the hostiles are closing fast. Don't be stupid, I can help keep them off us, buy us some time until the police arrive."

"Fuck you, Taft. We're not even fifteen minutes away from the precinct. They'll be here any minute." Dan stopped breathing when he heard the van screeching to a halt.

Myra kicked the back of his seat. "We don't have a minute, you're going to die in less than ten seconds if you don't pass me a gun. Those men want me and Jamilah alive. They don't give a damn about you."

"Even if I wanted to give you a gun, I couldn't," Dan said in a shaky voice. "By the time I pull my keys out the ignition, find the cuff key, and then fumble around to uncuff you—"

Myra reached her hand around his seat and tapped him on the shoulder. "I'm uncuffed, pass me the gun."

"How did you—"

"Really, Dan? A pair of standard handcuffs? You may as well had tied a ribbon with a bow on my wrists." She tapped his shoulder again. "Gun… Now!"

Dan placed the forty-five caliber in her hand. "Now what, Miss Special Forces?"

"On my count, you fire at the men in front of us, I'll fire at the one behind us, and then we get out of this Hummer."

"What? Wait. If we flee from the Hummer, they'll shoot us."

"Keep Jamilah close to you, they might not be so quick to fire."

"Your plan sucks, it sounds like suicide," Dan spat out.

"Do you have a better one?" Myra countered. Dan was silent. "Didn't think so." Myra flipped the safety off the forty-five, and then grabbed the door handle. "Get ready to move on my mark."

Walker had been following the Hummer from a distance. As the Hummer reached the ambush point he and Cleary decided the best spot to snatch Myra from the agents, he watched in shock as a blue van fishtailed to a halt. Three men with ski masks and automatic weapons jumped out and opened fire on the Hummer. He smashed on his brakes and grabbed his Uzi from under the passenger seat.

He exited his car and crouched behind the driver's door and aimed in the gunmen's general direction. He had two problems. One, the Hummer was in his line of fire. Two, Uzis weren't long-range weapons. There was no way his bullets were going to accurately reach the gunmen from where he was. Just as he was about to move from behind the car door and advance closer, the Hummer's reverse lights lit up and the Hummer lurched backward. He watched as the gunmen jumped back in the van and chased the Hummer down.

Walker looked over his shoulder. He could hear the faint sounds of police sirens. Now, he had three problems to deal with. Make that four. The Hummer changed course and was on a collision course right for him. Problem four led into problem five. Now, that the gunmen were chasing down the Hummer, the bullets that missed the Hummer were now coming at him. He flinched as two bullets ricocheted off the hood of his car. Two more tore into his windshield, cracking it in two places.

Walker took a deep breath and concentrated. He couldn't shoot around the Hummer at the gunmen; so he braced himself as he prepared to shoot through the Hummer's rear and front windshields.

"Don't shoot the inside of their vehicle!" The driver of the van said in Arabic. "Only shoot at their tires; we can't risk Jamilah getting shot."

The gunmen continued shooting at the Hummer's tires and grille. The van driver instinctively swerved when a bullet hit the van's windshield. He looked at the Hummer and saw no one. Who was firing at them?

"Look!" one of the gunmen said, pointing at the Hummer. "It's slowing down."

"Ah!" the van driver yelled out as a bullet grazed his hand.

"They're firing at us," one of the gunmen said to the driver. The gunman stopped aiming at the Hummer's tires and aimed higher, hoping to shoot whoever was shooting at them from inside the Hummer.

"No!" the van driver said, as he slammed on the brakes. "Jamilah must not be harmed." The van fishtailed to a halt.

"There!" the van driver said, pointing to the lone gunman behind the Hummer. "He is the one firing at us. Kill him."

"What about the Hummer?" one of the gunmen asked.

"They are pinned in by our gunfire. Kill that disbeliever, then we will handle the ones in the Hummer. Hurry! Time is not on our side."

The van's side door slid open and the gunmen jumped out."

"Let's do this!" Myra yelled, as she kicked open the Hummer door.

Dan followed suit, kicking his door open and diving on the ground. Myra took aim at Walker as Dan aimed at the three masked gunmen advancing toward them. They both fired at their targets. Myra's bullets ripped through the hood of Walker's car. Her last two bullets penetrated the driver's car door before embedding themselves into his bullet proof vest.

The three masked gunmen scattered for cover when Dan started shooting in their direction. One of the gunmen grabbed the right side of his ribcage where one of Dan's bullets penetrated. The driver of the van jumped out, dragging an AK-47 in tow.

"Gun!" Dan yelled, as the van driver swung the AK in their direction.

Myra whipped her head around. When she saw the AK, she understood why Dan yelled gun. The AK-47 was one of the few guns in the world that could shoot *through* almost anything. Myra joined Dan in directing her fire at the van driver. They couldn't allow him to get a single shot off. Not until they were safely tucked behind something the AK couldn't penetrate; and now, there wasn't anything in the vicinity that fit the bill.

The van driver kept walking toward Dan and Myra as if he was bullet proof. His arm came up, the nozzle of the AK locked onto the space between Dan's eyes. Dan dived into the Hummer. Myra blocked out everything and focused her last bullets on the imaginary bull's eye on the van driver's chest.

"Ah!" the van driver yelled. Myra's bullet hit him in the arm, causing his whole body to twist out of the line of fire of the two bullets that followed. The first bullet actually saved his life. The two that followed were on a direct course for his forehead.

"Let's go!" Myra yelled into the Hummer.

"Go where?" Dan yelled. "We're pinned in from both sides."

"We just can't—" Myra words got caught in her throat as she looked up and saw another man jump out of the van dragging an AK. It wasn't the AK that kept her eyes glued to him. It was who he was.

"Hassan." She said just above a whisper.

His whole body tensed as he locked eyes with Myra. He flipped the safety off the AK and pulled the trigger. Myra blindly shot in his direction as she dived into the Hummer. The AK bullets punched fist-sized holes in the open hummer doors.

Myra snuck a peek over one of the seats and saw Hassan walking toward the Hummer. Two of the other gunmen flanked him. The two gunmen separated, one going left, the other right, when they came within 20 yards of the Hummer. They each kept their guns trained on Walker as they advanced. Myra had been in enough battles to know when the end was near. The Hummer was now a death trap and there was no escaping it. She chanced a look out the back window and saw Walker steadily retreating behind car after car. He was making sure to keep a safe distance. Myra saw Dan squirming in the front seat of the Hummer. He kept looking over his left and right shoulder. Myra imagined a devil on his left telling him to jump out the Hummer and take as many out as he could before going down in a hail of bullets while the angel on his right was telling him to stay put and rely on the mercy of his attackers. The snarl on Dan's face told Myra that the devil was making more sense to Dan.

She placed a hand on his shoulder. "Don't do it."

Dan swatted her hand away. "If I'm going to die, I'm going to die on my terms."

Jamilah snapped out of her shock and reached out to grab Dan to keep him in the Hummer, but he'd already slithered out and was on his feet. Dan got off one shot before all three men turned their guns on him and filled him with bullets. Jamilah's screams stopped the gunfire.

"Jamilah," Hassan called out as he cautiously approached the Hummer.

Jamilah curled into a ball on the front seat and hugged herself tight to keep herself from shaking.

Myra looked down at the .45 in her hand. The slide was locked back, indicating the gun was empty. Out manned, out gunned. Myra bit her bottom lip. All possibilities of leaving this battlefield today were null except one.

"Jamilah," Myra said, as she poked her. Jamilah muffled her cries as she worked up the courage to glance back at Myra. "You and I both know that Hassan isn't going to let any harm come to you, so you're going to have to trust me, okay?"

"Trust you how?"

Myra slithered over the seat. She released the slide of the gun so the barrel could slide back in place and then grabbed Jamilah by her hair, and yanked her out of the Hummer. Hassan and his gunmen turned their guns on Myra. Myra kept Jamilah in front of her.

"In order to shoot me, you have to shoot through her," Myra yelled at Hassan.

"Don't," Hassan said turning to the gunmen. He then turned his gaze toward Myra. "Let her go and I will let you go."

"I'll let her go when I'm a safe distance away from you and your men." Myra tightened her grip on Jamilah's neck. Jamilah gasped.

Hassan started to run toward her and skidded in his tracks as Myra stuck the .45 under Jamilah's chin.

"I will blow her head clean off her shoulders," Myra said backing up a little.

"She's innocent," Hassan said. "How can you do this to her. She saved your life in Iraq? Have you no conscience, demon?"

"You do know that conscience and demon don't even sound right in the same sentence, right?"

Police sirens wailed in the background. Myra smiled, Hassan snarled.

"Here comes the Calvary," Myra mused.

The gunmen started talking to Hassan in rapid Arabic. They were trying to convince him to get into the van and deal with the demon another day.

"Listen to them," Myra said starting to laugh.

Hassan turned to her with rage in his eyes and then threw Myra for a loop with his snarl turned to a smile. Soon he was laughing. Myra arched a brow.

"He's lost it," she whispered in Jamilah's ear. Myra jammed the .45 harder under Jamilah's neck. Jamilah gasped and then busted out laughing. Myra craned her neck and looked into Jamilah's face.

"I'm sorry," Jamilah said. "But I have to end this."

Myra's eyes bulged as she felt Jamilah grab the inside of her thumb and quickly dislodge the .45 out of her hand. Before Myra had a chance to react, Jamilah had already ducked under Myra's arm while still holding the inside of her thumb. When Jamilah got behind her, she kicked Myra in the right kidney, dropping her to one knee. In the blink of an eye, Myra went from using Jamilah as a human shield with a gun under her chin to a shocked prisoner having the wind kicked out of her. Myra winced as she looked up at Jamilah.

"No fucking way."

"Yes, fucking way." Jamilah's smile turned into a jagged snarl as she brought the .45 crashing down on Myra's head. The last thing Myra saw before her head hit the street was Hassan and his gunmen firing in the direction of Walker.

CHAPTER 13

*I*n the beginning…

Shindand Airbase, located in southwest Afghanistan, a Blackhawk helicopter made its descent. The side door slid open just as the wheels of the helicopter hit the landing strip. A woman in full Muslim garb hopped off and walked toward Major Jennings who was sitting in the back of a jeep waiting for her.

"What are you doing here?" the woman said, as she approached the jeep. The woman's face was covered except for the slits for her eyes, but the attitude in her voice was unmistakable.

Jennings gave her the eye Myra knew all too well, indicating that at this moment he wasn't her surrogate father and she needed to respect his rank in front of other Army personnel. Myra removed the headwear, eyed the soldier on the driver's side of the jeep and then looked back at Jennings.

"What are you doing here… Major?" Myra added his rank but kept the attitude.

"Hop in," Jennings said, as he shook his head.

They rode in the back of the jeep in silence as the MP drove them to a hanger that had been converted into an ad hock of offices. Myra and Jennings entered an office isolated from the rest, a sign indicating to Myra things were going to be said that Jennings didn't want anyone to hear.

"It's been a while," Jennings said, as he casually walked around the office. "So, how's CST treating you?" CST stood for Cultural Support Team. Major Jennings went toe-to-toe with the Army's top brass and persuaded them to allow him to put together a small unit of women soldiers to serve with front-line combat units in some of the most specialized and covert missions. The Cultural Support Team was attached to Special Forces and Ranger units to interface with the female population in hostile regions to gain vital intelligence and provide social outreach. Some of the female soldiers wore Army fatigues while some, due to some of the hostile neighborhoods they patrolled with Special Forces, wore traditional Muslim garb.

Myra folded her arms. "Don't—"

"Okay, okay," Jennings said. "Let me stop acting like my visit is a social one."

"Because it's not," Myra said.

"Because it's not," Jennings repeated. "I've been given the go-ahead to initiate the M.O.P. program."

"Official or unofficial?"

"Listen, Myra, you know my ways are unorthodox."

"You give unorthodox a whole new meaning."

"We're not going to win new wars with old strategies, and it's going to take some of the old warhorses in the Pentagon another twenty years to realize that."

"Okay, so this mission is unofficial. What about the other women?"

"They're not ready, they'll remain on the CST."

"What do you mean they're not ready?"

"Their progress reports since being on CST have been minimal."

"Meaning?"

"Meaning it's hard to turn a nurturer by nature into a heartless killer." Jennings saw when Myra arched her eyebrow. "I'm not saying that you're a heartless killer... you're just closer to being one than the others."

"Wow, I don't know if I should be honored or hurt."

"C'mon, Myra, you know what I'm trying to say."

"But I don't know what you're trying to do. What's the purpose of this unofficial project?" Jennings looked around the office. "No one can hear us, you made sure we came into an office separated from the rest."

"Never could be too careful," Jennings said with a jittery smile.

"So?" Myra prompted.

"You and two other soldiers have been chosen to become the weapon that's going to win the war on terror."

Myra chuckled. "Give it to me without the sales pitch."

"MOP's a deep infiltration unit; one that isn't restricted by rules, regulations, or morals."

"How deep?"

"You will do whatever's necessary to identify and locate the heads of the Arab terrorist networks and eliminate them with extreme prejudice."

"Just the Arabs?"

"For now, they're the focus."

"When you say no rules or regulations—"

"It means just that. You answer to no one. You do whatever you have to do. We're only interested in results. Whatever means you choose to get those results are of no concern to us."

"And who's us?"

"Really, Myra?"

"I just thought… being that you were so forthcoming with the info…"

Myra and Jennings turned toward the door when it opened.

"Gentlemen, come in," Major Jennings said to the two soldiers who stared Myra up and down as they stepped into the office. "Taft," Jennings said putting on his Major persona in front of the soldiers, "this is Cleary and this is Walker."

Myra looked them up and down. She knew Cleary and Walker weren't their real names any more than Taft was hers.

"Never worked with a woman before," Walker said.

"And you're not working with one now," Myra retorted.

"What she's saying, Walker," Cleary said, as he stared at Myra. "is in war there are no men or women, just soldiers. If you look at soldiers as men or women, you'll tend to under or overestimate them. Either way can get you killed. Am I right, Taft?"

"Somebody was paying attention in basic training. I bet you graduated at the top of your class," Myra said sarcastically.

"Actually, I got kicked out of basic training twice. Something about me having a problem with authority and getting along with others."

Myra looked at Jennings. "Still know how to pick 'em, huh?"

"I see the chemistry between you guys already," Jennings said.

"Yeah, the chemistry for nitroglycerin," Myra said.

"If this doesn't work," Walker began, "if this unit doesn't win the war on terror, and the particulars of this unsanctioned unit somehow got leaked, we'll be branded traitors by our country. The President himself will order our immediate execution."

"They can't kill three people who are already dead, right Major?" Walker said.

"Dead?" Myra said.

"I see you didn't graduate at the top of your class," Cleary said smiling. "With the atrocities we're about to commit, there's no way we can ever be linked to the United States. All records of our existence will be erased."

"Wrong, Sergeant," Jennings said. "All records of your existence are in tact. You guys did very much exist."

"Did?" Myra said.

"I regret to have to inform you, but you guys died in a training accident two hours ago, so enough talk," Jennings said turning serious. "We have terrorists to kill."

The Present...

Myra's eyes fluttered as she slowly came to. She was in total darkness except for the occasional slither of light that flickered from the bottom of the hood that had been put over her head. She winced as she shifted her weight in the metal chair. She could tell by the stiffness of her joints and the involuntary twitches of her heroin-deprived body that she had been unconscious for hours. The handcuffs interlaced through the metal chair's back in order to restrain her hands behind her back clanked as she tried freeing herself. Myra stopped struggling when she heard footsteps approaching. She heard snippets of rapid Arabic. The first voice she recognized was Hassan's. He was saying what they were about to do was a bad idea. The second voice she recognized was Jamilah's telling him he worries more than a pregnant woman. The next voice stopped her breathing, increased her heartbeat, and brought tears to her eyes.

The hood was yanked off her head, but she refused to open her eyes. In order to become an indiscriminate killing machine, you have to build a shield around your psyche and then further insulate it by burying it deep within the abyss of your subconscience where it is kept hidden from all of your wrong doing. That is the only way you won't go crazy. That's how the Army trained her, that's how the Army's unofficial special training camps in the Middle East trained Zakawi. He knew the only way to break a special ops soldier was to unbury their psyche and then get into it. For years he tried everything but death to get into Myra's but he failed—so he thought.

Zakawi smiled as he looked down at her in disdain. He saw the tears running down from the corners of her eyes, and the tremors just beneath her skin. He leaned down so he could be face-to-face with Myra, but she must've sensed his intentions and jerked back in the chair, sending her and the chair toppling over.

Zakawi let out a bellowing laugh and then looked to Hassan. "Get her up."

Hassan looked down at Myra as if she was a bug he was about to squash under his boot. He thought of the way she left him strung up in the basement of that school in Iraq. He reached down and with one hand grabbed the metal chair while the other clamped around her neck. He squeezed, praying to Allah to hear the sound of her neck snapping like a twig. He righted the chair with her in it, but his hand remained locked around her neck until Myra's eyes popped open.

"Hassan!" Jamilah called out.

Hassan blinked out of his rage-induced trance. He let go of Myra and stepped back, never once taking his eyes off her as she took in lungs full of air. Myra looked around for the first time and saw that she was in the center of a warehouse surrounded by Zakawi, Jamilah, Hassan, and the gunmen who had jumped out the van on them earlier.

Zakawi busted out laughing again. "I see Hassan still hasn't forgiven you for the way you left him in that basement."

Myra locked eyes with him. She was fully conscious now; back in battle mode, her psyche safely buried.

Zakawi leaned down until he was face-to-face with her. While Zakawi looked at her, he realized that Myra was looking through him. It sent a chill down his spine. He smiled when he felt it. He stood back up and took a step back.

"Still the same demon, I see."

"Still the same heartless terrorist, I see," Myra said, jerking on the handcuffs, indicating that every time they met he always made sure she was restrained.

Zakawi smiled again. This time it was an uneasy smile. A smile indicating that he knew he was about to do something he knew he shouldn't, but felt he had to in order to save face. "Remove the handcuffs," he said to Hassan.

"Zaka—" Hassan started to say.

"I *said* remove them."

Hassan dug out the cuff key and reluctantly walked behind Myra and removed the handcuffs. Myra winced as she brought her hands to rest on her lap. She observed how the gunmen from the van subtly wrapped their trigger fingers around the triggers of the AKs hanging from their necks. Zakawi saw it as well and held his hand up to his men.

The gunmen looked at Zakawi and one by one they removed their fingers off the triggers of their AKs.

Zakawi nodded in approval and then looked back at Myra. "I must admit," Zakawi said while taking a step closer to Myra, "I never used to listen to Jamilah when it came to strategy. Look at her," he said, pointing to her. "She's young, she's beautiful... what could youth and beauty possibly know about war?" Jamilah walked up to Zakawi and slid her arm around his waist and looked deep into his eyes. Then they shared a passionate kiss.

Myra flashed back to that night when her and the team raided Zakawi's house to kill him, to the moment when she had her knife to Jamilah's neck and asked her who she was to Zakawi. *I am his daughter,* Jamilah had said. The Intel on Zakawi never mentioned a daughter, only a mother and... a wife. Myra replayed it scene by scene. Demon one had threatened to impale Jamilah with the splintered end of a stick, but Zakawi's wife still refused to tell them where Zakawi was. A mother, knowing what was about to happen to her daughter, would've told. Even if she didn't know, she would've made something up, would've said anything to save her child. Yet, she held out. Myra now knew why. She was Zakawi's wife… but she wasn't his only wife.

Zakawi broke the lip lock and whispered something to Jamilah that made her giggle. She looked at Myra and her face turned stone.

"I could not understand that night why she stopped me from killing you," Zakawi said. "I was going to put a bullet through your mouth, but something inside me wouldn't let me close my finger over the trigger, and for the first time, I listened to Jamilah. Later, she explained to me that you and one of the other demons fought over what he was about to do to her. After much persuasion, she convinced me to keep you alive, convinced me that you were the one we have been looking for." Zakawi chuckled. "The one that our people have been praying for."

"Praying for?" Myra said with a disgusted look.

"My people believe that the only way Allah will destroy the Devil is with one of his own."

Myra shook her head.

"It's true," Jamilah said. "You were one of them, yet, you didn't allow them to harm me. You don't fight for your country, you fight for what's right."

Myra turned away from her.

Jamilah moved to kneel by Myra, but Hassan quickly stepped in front of her. Jamilah tried to push past him, but he held his ground. The handcuffs had been removed from Myra. He knew what Myra was capable of.

"Hassan, move," Jamilah said. "She will not harm me." Hassan didn't move. Jamilah looked toward Zakawi. He reluctantly waved his hand at Hassan for him to move out the way. Hassan moved so Jamilah could kneel next Myra.

"You know what I'm saying is true. I heard you talk in your sleep about getting even, about killing them all." Myra tried to turn her head. Jamilah grabbed her by the chin and held her gaze. "You know what I'm saying is true."

"It's true," Myra growled. "But when I strike, it will be by myself and they will know it's me."

"Strike?" Zakawi said. "Strike with what? Ashraf and the rest of the members of the cell along with their cache of artillery have been taken into custody. Any chances you had of getting your revenge have been rendered moot with Ashraf's arrest."

Myra's leg began to shake. Zakawi took it as a sign that Myra was beginning to crack.

"Blowing up the UN was a decoy."

"Jennings told me."

"Jennings?" Zakawi looked shocked.

"Yes, he knows about the UN bombing plan and that it's a decoy."

"That old man never ceases to amaze me. He may have known about Ashraf's mission, but he doesn't know mine."

"And how do you know he doesn't?"

"Trust me, I know."

"So, what is your mission?" Myra asked.

"Not my mission; *your* mission. You're going to murder the President of the United States."

Myra busted out laughing. "You must be high."

Zakawi walked toward her and stopped within arm's distance. "Do I look high to you?"

Myra stopped laughing.

"I'm offering you a chance to change the course of history. Not with a bomb or from a far off distance through a sniper's scope, but with your bare-hands." Zakawi looked down at Myra's leg. The twitch in it was becoming more pronounced and then he noticed the beads of sweat forming on her head. He smiled realizing that it had been hours since Myra had a hit. He held out his hand toward Jamilah. Jamilah reached in her jacket and retrieved a tiny Ziploc bag filled with heroin and handed it to him.

"Demon," Zakawi said as he tossed the bag to her.

Myra snatched it out the air like a frog's tongue wrapped around a fly. She brought her cravings under control and looked around at everyone, one by one.

"Go ahead, demon," Zakawi said, "we won't judge you."

Myra glanced at the bag and then looked back at each of them. She tossed the bag to Jamilah. "I don't want anything from you."

Jamilah slowly walked up to Myra and twirled the bag between her fingers. She smiled as Myra's eyes followed the bag's flipping and rotating motions.

"You know you want it," Jamilah said, as she teasingly opened the bag. "No? Ok." She slowly tipped the bag threatening to empting its contents on the floor. Myra's hand shot out and snatched the bag out of Jamilah's hand before a single particle fell from the bag. Zakawi smiled as Myra poured the heroin out onto the back of her hand and sniffed it.

Myra's eye rolled to the back of her head as she slumped into the chair. Ten seconds later, her eyes popped open and she sat straight up.

"How are you feeling?" Zakawi asked.

"Better," Myra said with a euphoric smile.

Zakawi's smile broadened. "Now, where were we?"

Myra held her hand up, thought for a moment, and then snapped her fingers. "Me killing the President of the United States."

"Yes," Zakawi said, "you killing the President of the United States."

CHAPTER 14

*T*he Director of Special Ops, Peter Folks, stood in the windowless Roosevelt Room in the White House waiting for the President to show up for their appointed meeting.

"Peter," the President said, as he walked in and shook Folks's hand.

"Mr. President," Folks said, as they both sat.

"So, tell me what's this all about?"

"Mr. President, we've uncovered a terrorist plot to bomb the UN this Friday where you were scheduled to give your speech."

"Has anyone been arrested?"

"No."

"So, there's nothing to worry about, then. Has this gone public yet?"

"I would suggest that it shouldn't. The American people are still recovering from 9/11."

The President nodded. "I agree. Good work, Peter. Is there anything else I should know?"

"There was one other thing. One of our own was suspected to be involved. An Army Major."

"What? Has this been confirmed?"

"No, Mr. President. He's been under investigation for the past six months after he was seen with one of the men on Homeland Security's watch list."

"Where is this Major?"

"Mr. President," Folks said, submissively. "that information is above my security clearance."

The President waved his hand. "Yes, yes, I understand." The President folded one leg over the other and thought for a moment. "Has the threat been thoroughly eliminated?"

Folks hesitated before he spoke. "Mr. President, if I may, I believe you should cancel the meeting with the P.O.W. soldier we recently rescued from Iraq."

"What? From what I was told, he underwent the most gruesome of torture imaginable. And he did it for his country. What would the American people say if I didn't personally welcome this heroic soldier home? The members of our armed forces and the American people need to know that their service is invaluable to our freedom and that this Presidency will forever be grateful for their sacrifices. The least I can do is welcome this young man home."

"Yes, Mr. President, I understand, however, maybe if you did it in a more secure environment or an undisclosed location."

"Peter. I will be welcoming that soldier home tomorrow at Fort Bragg when that chopper lands. And that's the end of it. If Fort Bragg isn't secure enough, then we have bigger problems than I thought."

"Yes, Mr. President. I apologize for—"

"Don't apologize, help us win this war on terror."

"Yes, Mr. President," Folks said, as he got up. Both men stood and shook hands.

Peter Folks walked to his car struggling not to immediately pull out his phone to make the call. He waited until he drove a few miles away from The White House before dialing the number.

"Yes," the man on the line said.

"Tomorrow, Fort Bragg."

"The way you extract information from him amazes me," Zakawi said. "He knows not to tell anyone his itinerary, yet, he tells it to you."

"He tells it to me, because he doesn't realize that he's telling it to me. Everything set?"

"Everything overseas is set. Just tying up a few loose ends on this side."

"Do it quickly. There's no margin for error."

"Don't worry, by the end of the day, we will have a new leader."

Myra shifted in the metal chair, straining her neck to see where Zakawi had gone. Whoever just called him must've been important for him to leave his conversation with her about killing the President. She already surmised he had someone high up the ladder to know for certain that Jennings didn't know about his plans. A few moments later he returned smiling. Myra started to rub her knees. "You don't mind if I get up and stretch my legs, do you?" she said to Zakawi.

"Be my guest, but I warn you, demon, my men don't trust you, so no sudden movements."

Myra stood up. "And what about you, do you trust me?"

"I trust that you'll do the right thing."

"Do you now?"

"Yes, I do."

"So, how in the world am I going to get close enough to the President to murder him?"

"You're going to walk into the White House and kill him."

Myra laughed. "I'm just going to walk into the White House? No one just walks into the White House."

"You will. And they won't even suspect a thing."

Myra laughed and stumbled backward. The gunmen tensed.

"Demon," Zakawi said. "You underestimate determination. Anything can be done if you're determined and patient enough. I've had eyes on you since you made it back to the States, demon. *Every* move you've made has been guided by me."

"Really?" Myra said.

"Really. Is it a coincidence that your therapist just happened to be the sister of an American soldier I've held captive for over 18 months?"

Myra stopped smiling. "Was it a coincidence that you met up with a heroin dealer in a bar?" Zakawi winked at Jamilah and then looked back to Myra. "It was Jamilah's idea to hook you and Omar up."

"Omar's been buying product from our distributors for years," Jamilah said. "When I pointed you out to him in the bar the night he introduced himself to you, he said he knew that you would be a challenge, but he never met a woman strong enough to resist The White Knight."

Myra cocked her head as she thought back to the night Omar walked up on her. In her mind she traced the direction from which he came, and there, in a booth, she remembered seeing a woman in a business suit, sipping on a drink, taking care to conceal her face with the brim of her lace hat.

"Lace hat, white silk dress shirt, two top buttons undone," Myra said aloud.

Jamilah nodded, amazed at Myra's memory.

Myra shook her head. "No."

"Yes," Zakawi said. "Your whole time back, we were watching you, testing you, waiting for the right moment to approach you."

"Bullshit. There was no way you could've known that the drug deal in my house was going to go down the way it did."

"An unforeseen event that only forced us to act now rather than later."

"Killing the President won't stop what's going on in your country. The VP will take over and it will be business as usual."

"It will be business, but it won't be as usual."

"I can't believe you went through all of this to... to test me," Myra said.

"Like Jamilah said," Zakawi said, "our people thought you were the chosen one. As for me, I needed a little more convincing."

"And are you convinced?" Myra asked.

Zakawi smiled and then whispered something to Hassan. Hassan ran up a metal staircase to an office that overlooked the whole warehouse. He came out with a body over his shoulder. It was Laura. Hassan dropped Laura at the feet of Myra. Laura was gagged with her hands bound behind her back. She looked up at Myra through teary eyes.

Zakawi removed his 9mm from his shoulder holster and then removed the clip from it before tossing the 9mm to Myra. "There's one in the head."

Myra slid the barrel back half way and saw the single bullet in the chamber. She looked down at Laura and then looked toward Zakawi.

"Well, demon?" he said.

Myra knelt down beside Laura and put the gun to the side of Laura's head. "Give me a countdown, Hassan," Myra said without looking up at him.

"What?" Hassan said dumbfounded.

"Count down from five... in English."

"I don't see why—"

"Just do it," Zakawi snapped at Hassan.

Hassan sighed. "Five, four, three two."

The gunmen crumpled to the ground, each had blood oozing from their heads. Before Zakawi, Jamilah, and Hassan could fully understand what was going on, the warehouse turned pitch black.

"Demon!" Zakawi yelled out as Hassan fired in the spot Myra and Laura had been seconds ago. "I will kill you, demon you hear me?"

Myra's arm slipped around Zakawi's neck. "Loud and clear."

As the lights flickered back on, Hassan and Jamilah nearly jumped out of their skins when they saw Demon One and Demon Two with M-16s advancing toward them.

"Allahu Akbar (Allah's the Greatest)," Hassan shouted before he raised his gun. Cleary squeezed off one shot as Walker kept his M-16 trained on Jamilah. Hassan fell to the ground with a gaping hole in his chest. Jamilah let out a piercing scream and raised her gun at Myra. Myra shoved the gun she had with only one bullet against Zakawi's head.

"One of two things is going to happen, Jamilah," Myra said. "Either you're going to fire that gun and shoot your husband or you going to shoot me, which in turn, is going to make me pull this trigger and blow his head off."

"She's bluffing," Zakawi said to Jamilah. "If they wanted us dead, they would've killed us already; they want us alive, they need us alive." Zakawi smiled when he saw Cleary and Walker lower their weapons. "See, my love? They're not going to kil—"

Myra squeezed off her single round.

"No!" Zakawi screamed as he watched blood spurt from Jamilah's eye. Jamilah's body hit the floor with a sickening thud.

Zakawi turned on Myra and tried to grab her by her neck, but Myra had already back peddled out of reach. Zakawi ran to Jamilah's corpse and cradled her head in his arms. "No!" He turned to Myra and stared at her with a madman's glare.

"I am going to kill you." He jumped to his feet and charged Myra. Myra sidestepped his advance and kicked him in the right knee. Zakawi grunted and dropped to one knee.

"The infamous Zakawi," Myra taunted. "Crying like a little bitch."

"Ahhh!" Zakawi yelled as he charged Myra again. Myra grappled with him and then kicked him in the same exact spot on his right knee. Zakawi rolled around on the ground as he held his knee.

"That's it?" Myra taunted.

Zakawi winced as he stood up. He kept the majority of his weight on his left leg. He put his hands up like a boxer. "C'mon," he said, beckoning Myra to attack.

Myra circled him like a hawk. With each circle, she stepped in, until she finally attacked. Zakawi blocked her punches and wised up to the kick to the right knee and protected it. He slipped a punch in to Myra's jaw that backed her up. Zakawi kept on the offense. He threw a whirlwind of punches. He backed Myra up against a wooden crate. He finally got his hand around her neck. Myra clawed at his hand and arm, and then threw punches at his face.

"I'm going to snap your neck, demon, like I should've done years ago."

"You couldn't kill me then," Myra struggled to talk, "and you can't kill me now." Myra gritted her teeth and kicked him in the balls with all her might.

Zakawi doubled over but refused to let go of Myra's neck. Zakawi bending down allowed Myra to drop to the ground on her back. She grabbed the hand that Zakawi had around her neck and quickly snaked her legs around his neck forming a figure four leg-lock choke hold. Myra used Zakawi's arm along with her legs to choke him out. Zakawi's grip loosened around Myra's neck as he started to gasp for air.

"Demon," Zakawi choked out, as he focused on her eyes.

Myra looked him in the eyes. "Everything *you* saw was meant for you to see." In that moment, Zakawi saw the whole playback in the pupils of Myra's eyes. The Ex Special Ops, dope fiend, suffering from Post-Traumatic Stress Disorder was just one of the many characters in Myra's array of identities. The whole time he'd been watching her, introducing people in her life to control her, she was the one who was actually in control.

He strained to look up at Cleary and Walker who were witnessing his slow death. Zakawi looked down at Myra and tried one last attempt at breaking the hold, but he was too weak and light-headed to do anything but stare in her eyes as his lids slowly began to close.

Myra held onto him until the last breath of air left his lungs and his body went limp. She kicked him off of her and tried to stand. Cleary and Walker ran to her aid and each grabbed her by an arm.

"You okay?" Cleary asked.

Myra nodded weakly. "We don't have much time."

"Time?" Cleary said. "What do you mean?"

"Zakawi's full of shit. He never had any plans on using me to assassinate the President. Zakawi is the master of decoys and distractions. He never hits his intended target head on. He always creates a distraction to get everyone to scramble away from the target."

"So, the President isn't the target?" Cleary asked.

"He's the target, he's just not going to be attacked at the White House."

"If not at the White House and by you," Walker asked, "then where and by who?"

Myra looked over at Laura who had been sitting against a crate dumbfounded. Laura still couldn't wrap her mind around seeing Myra, Cleary, and Walker together working as a team.

"C'mon, Doc," Myra said to Laura. "You have a President to save."

CHAPTER 15

F ort Bragg. Home of the Airborne and Special Operations Forces. The welcoming committee awaiting Private Randal's arrival was fit for a General. The President, Vice President, Director of Special Operations, and Secretary of Defense were in attendance, as were soldiers from the different branches, and T.V. crews. Everyone started clapping when they saw the helicopter approaching. As the chopper landed, the door slid open and out stepped Laura's brother timidly. The applause swelled to a deafening thunder of claps.

Laura's brother, David, didn't move from the side of the chopper. The helicopter co-pilot stepped out and put his arm around him and gently walked him toward the crowd of well-wishers. Laura's brother glanced down at the co-pilot's sidearm. He licked his lips as he tried to steady his breathing. His heartbeat increased with each step he took toward the President. He shut out the present and retreated into his mind; back to the pleasant memories that gave him solace. Back to the evenings when Jamilah would come see him after a day of grueling torture. She was allowed to come see him once every three days to bathe him. After a few months, she began to sneak him food and drink. On his fourth month, he cracked. He told Zakawi everything he wanted to know. Everything from his personal life, to basic training, to the little Army intelligence he had. Zakawi had given the one they called Hassan the order to kill him and feed him to the dogs at nightfall.

David tried not to breakdown and cry when Hassan shackled his arms and legs and dumped him in the back of a truck to take him out to the desert. The ride to the desert was worse than death itself. All David could think of was Hassan slitting his throat with that humongous knife he always brandished and then leaving his corpse for the wild dogs to rip apart.

When the truck finally stopped, David opened his eyes and realized that they weren't in the desert but that they were in a deserted town. Hassan lifted him out of the truck and carried him to a dilapidated schoolhouse. Hassan chained him to a pipe in the basement and left. A few hours later, the weight of footsteps caused the rickety staircase that led to the basement to creak. David looked up and cried. Looking down at him was his angel—Jamilah.

David was pulled from his thoughts when the co-pilot escorting him toward the crowd tapped him on the shoulder and pointed toward the President. David mustered a weak smile and glanced down at the co-pilot's sidearm again. David judged that they were twenty yards away. Ten more yards and he would make his move.

Myra, Cleary, and Walker were strategically placed in the crowd of well-wishers. They wore army fatigues, caps pulled low to their eyes.

"If this doesn't play out the way you say," Cleary said to Myra through his Bluetooth, "we're dead."

"We're already dead," Myra responded through her Blue-tooth. "We died in a helicopter crash five years ago."

"Very funny," Cleary said, "for a dead person."

"Knock it off," Walker said through his Bluetooth. "He's about ten yards away, how much longer are we going to wait."

"Just wait," Myra said. "This is going to work, trust me." Myra heard Cleary sigh. "What?" she said.

"You know what."

"This is a delicate situation, which is why the Secretary said my course of action was the best for all parties involved."

"It's also the riskiest. There's no room for error."

"When have we ever made an error?"

Cleary got quiet.

"Exactly. So just get ready to move on my mark."

David had reached the ten yard mark, the point of no return. He looked down at the co-pilot's sidearm and reached for it.

"David!"

David looked up and froze. Laura slid from behind the President and ran toward him.

"Laura?"

"My God, David." Laura ran into his arms. She could feel his body soften as he wrapped his arms around her. Then just as quick as he softened, he hardened back up.

Laura tensed up as well. "You don't have to do this, you hear me?" David didn't respond. "They lied to you, David. The only reason why they released you was because they knew they had convinced you to do this. They lied to you."

Jamilah's beautiful face filled his mind's eye. She consoled him, she saved him from certain death, he heard Hassan telling her that if Zakawi knew that the soldier was still alive that he would kill him. David heard Jamilah telling Hassan that David was a good man. That he was going to save millions of lives by taking the life of one.

"No," David said, as he tried to pull away from Laura.

Laura held onto him for dear life. "Jamilah lied to you, David."

"Jamilah? How did you know about—"

"You're not the first soldier Jamiah and her husband, Zakawi, did this to. Please, David. Listen to me. I thought I lost you once. You do this and I *will* lose you."

David pulled away from her and stared at her. He shook his head, as his whole torturous ordeal flashed through his mind. Jamilah was his angel, she loved him. She spent plenty of nights in that school basement showing him how much she loved him. "You're lying." David took a few more steps away from her. "You're lying."

David's outburst caused a hush amongst the crowd.

"David—" Myra started to say.

"Get away from me."

"Sir," the co-pilot said.

David turned to him and remembered his mission. As David reached for the co-pilot's gun, the co-pilot back peddled and instinctive drew his sidearm. Cleary and Walker were already on the move. Cleary tackled David while Walker talked the co-pilot into lowering his weapon. Secret Service had the

President on the move; the crowd was filled with panic and shock. The only one calm was Myra. This was it. They were at the end game. She couldn't afford to make any mistakes. She kept her eyes on her target.

While everyone in the crowd looked around at each other in panic and shock, the Vice President and the Director of Special Operations looked at each other in disgust.

Myra's eyes widened. The name that Hassan had whispered to her, *Victor's Papa.* The name she overheard wasn't a real name. It was the Nato spelling alphabet; Alpha, Bravo, Charlie, Delta, etc. What Hassan heard was Victor Papa, VP, Vice President. The demons knew about Peter Folks and his involvement in a terrorist plot that was to take place on American soil. They discovered this intel from an insurgent they captured and tortured in Iraq. But what they *really* needed to know the insurgent couldn't tell them. They needed to know who else was involved. And the look that Folks and the Vice President shared told it all. The demons were never meant to fight the war on Terror on American soil, but Major Jennings had convinced someone high on the totem pole that only the demons were capable of flushing out all of the conspirators.

Myra flashed the Secretary of Defense a hand signal to which he nodded his acknowledgment.

After securing the President, the Secret Service's next priority was securing the Vice President. The Secretary of Defense grabbed the Vice President and Folks by their arms. Secret Service ushered them all to the Vice President's limo and shut the door.

"What the hell was that about?" the Vice President said to Folks and the Secretary of Defense who were sitting across from him in the spacious limo.

"Don't know," Folks responded.

The Vice President looked across at the Secretary of Defense. "You okay, Jack?"

"No, I'm not okay."

The Vice President smiled nervously. "It was probably nothing back there. You know how the Secret Service overreacts."

The Secretary of Defense smiled, but the look of disgust was evident in his eyes. Folks was the first to realize that the limo had turned onto a dirt road while their SUV escort in front of them kept straight along the highway.

"What's going on?"

The men looked at each other puzzled when they heard the door locks pop open. It was then that the Vice President realized that the driver wasn't his normal driver. And it was then that Folk's heart started to race. He knew the drill all too well. He just never imagined it would or that it could ever happen to him.

The backdoors swung open. Two men were on the right of the limo and one woman was on the left.

"God help me," Folks whispered when he saw Myra, Cleary, and Walker.

"God's on vacation," Myra said, as she shot Folks in the neck with a tranquilizer dart.

The Vice President's face turned beet red as he started hyperventilating. "Frank," he finally managed to say.

The Secretary of Defense calmly stepped out of the limo and straightened his tie. He then patted her on the shoulder. "You guys are as good as the Major said you were."

"How is he?" Myra asked.

"He's alive. I told him he's too old to be in the field."

"I tried to get him to sit this one out, but ..." Myra started to say.

"I know," the Secretary of Defense said. "He is a stubborn one."

"Frank," the Vice President yelled. "What the hell is going on?"

The Secretary of Defense looked at the demons, one by one. "You know what to do."

"Yes, Sir," they said in unison.

Cleary and Myra got into the back of the limo with the Vice President while Walker got in the driver's seat. The chauffer escorted the Secretary of Defense to the SUV Myra, Cleary, and Walker had followed them in and drove away.

The Vice President swallowed hard while looking at Cleary. Cleary looked like he was just waiting for the Vice President to open his mouth so he could stick his size 11 boot into it; so he turned to Myra.

"Young lady, I don't know what this is all about, but—"

"Mr. Vice President, Franklin Matthews. Heroic fighter pilot, shot down behind enemy lines during desert storm in 1992. Held captive for... what was it, two years? Did they shackle you face down on a rock in the middle of the desert where the temperature hits a hundred degrees and you literally smell your flesh cooking? And then at night when the temperature drops to thirty degrees, you go from your flesh being fried to your flesh being frozen. And how about the hours of being a punching bag for the little mujahideen in training…"

The beads of sweat that had formed on the Vice President's forehead ran down his face and started forming a stain ring on his collar. "Okay, someone gave you access to my debriefing file."

"Ooh," Myra said snapping her fingers, "What about their dart throwing tournaments? Yeah, you know what I'm talking about. The night watchmen would smoke their hashish and then start talking shit and then when they got bored, they would string you up and use you as a human dartboard. I bet you told them that in your debriefing, as well"

The Vice President nodded weakly.

"Let's talk about the things you didn't tell the shrinks. Let's talk about Zakawi."

The Vice President's face went from beet red to ghostly white as all the blood drained from his face.

"Yeah," Myra said, liking the reaction she got. "Let's talk about the caves and how they would stretch you across a boulder, shackle you down to it and whip you until your blood turned the boulder red."

The Vice President's eyes widened. "How did you know about the—"

"Your brain was mush, you had no sense of time, couldn't distinguish day from night. You probably didn't even know what country you were in. You were at the point of going insane."

The Vice President's lips began to quiver.

"You know how insanity feels, don't you? You're spinning out of control, reaching out trying to find something, anything to grab a hold to. And just when you were on the brink of passing the point of no return, lying in your own piss, shit, and blood, you look up and there... you see it. An angel. She cleaned you up, snuck you food and water, and stood up to the night watchmen."

The Vice President's lip started to quiver.

"Everyone abandoned you; your unit, your country, your God, everyone... except—"

"She saved me!" the Vice President said, spittle flying out of his mouth. "My country left me for dead. I prayed to God every day, every night, I prayed until they beat me unconscious. *He* forsook me, as well."

"But she didn't."

"No, she didn't. Zakawi broke me. Two months of torture and I broke. He picked me for everything I knew and then just like that, He told his men to take me out to the desert—"

"And feed you to the dogs."

"She convinced one of the men—"

"To bring you to an abandoned building where she nursed you back to health."

"She gave me my life back."

"She brained washed you."

The Vice President lunged for Myra. Cleary shoved the Vice President back into his seat.

"Move again, I'll kill you," Cleary said with no emotion.

Myra shook her head. "How did you think this was going to play out? The President gets assassinated, you become President and then what?"

The Vice President busted out laughing. "So, how's *this* going to play out?" he said, pointing at Folks, Cleary, and then to Myra. "Am I going to be put on trial for treason? No, I don't think so. You going to kill me?"

"No," Myra said.

The Vice President smiled. "Of course you're not. This is America, you're not stupid."

"No, Mr. Vice President," Myra said. "We're not stupid. We're Demons."

Cleary lunged at the Vice President and clamped his hands around his neck. The Vice President gripped and clawed at Cleary's fingers. Cleary's grip tightened around his neck. The Vice President's arms fell to his side. Myra tapped Cleary.

"I know, I know," Cleary said, as he sat back down.

Myra reached across and felt for the Vice President's pulse. It was faint, but it was there. She looked over at Peter Folks and shook her head. "I never thought we would have to use our skills here in America," she said to Cleary. "It's sad."

"This is what we do," Cleary said. "We go after the bad guys, whoever they may be; wherever they may be."

Myra stared out the window at the passing trees.

"Hey," Cleary said in a low voice. "This might not be the time, but..." He cleared his throat. "What we do isn't easy. Our existence depends on results. As team leader, it's my job to get those results. In the field I have to constantly evaluate our situation and make decisions."

Myra looked at him.

Cleary averted her gaze. "Back in Iraq, I did what I was trained to do, what we were trained to do."

"You left me for dead."

"At the rate you were losing blood, you're chances of surviving was next to none; and even if we could've stopped the bleeding, you would've slowed us down and possibly have gotten us all killed."

Myra stared at the limo's ceiling as she spoke, "If you had a chance to do it all over, would you make the same decision?"

Cleary put his head down.

"Wow," Myra said.

Cleary reached out to her. Myra knocked his hand away and turned to look out the window again. "Well... team leader, do your job and make the call."

"Myra—"

"Make the call."

Cleary pulled out a satellite phone and placed a call. "Packages will be delivered on schedule... yes... Thank you, Sir, but none of this could've happened without the invaluable Intel from one of our own... Yes, she truly is amazing." Cleary ended the call. "The SOD (Secretary of Defense) said he never saw a mission this sensitive handled with such surgical precision."

Myra kept looking out the window. Tomorrow the President will address the nation. He will sound broken up as he tells the American people that Franklin Carter Matthews who served his country as a fighter pilot, then as a congressman, then as Vice President of The United States died of a massive heart attack in his home. Three days later, the headlines of every paper in the country will run the story of the how the Director of Special Operations lost control of his car and drove off a cliff.

Of course there will be many conspiracy theories surrounding the sudden deaths of the Vice President and the Director of Special Operations, but that's all they'll be.

CHAPTER 16

L aura sat at her desk making notes in the margin of her pad about the client who just left her office. She looked at her phone when it rang. She absentmindedly answered it. "Dr. Randal."

"What's up, Doc?"

Laura's grip tightened around the receiver. "Myra?"

"Surprised to hear from me?"

Laura didn't respond.

"Just want to let you know that your brother is fine. He's getting the help he needs. Major Jennings is personally overseeing his care. He's been diagnosed with Post-Traumatic Stress Disorder."

"When can I see him?"

"I don't know. But the Major will let you know. I have to go."

"Myra, wait."

Myra ended the call just as Major Jennings walked into his office.

He pointed his cane at Myra and then pointed to the couch. "Sit."

"You know that's not happening."

Major Jennings shook his head and made his way to his desk. Myra approached to help him. He waved his cane at her.

"Come any closer and I'll whack you."

"I should've never allowed you to work this mission with us," Myra said.

Major Jennings sucked his teeth. "Last I checked, *I* decide who works what mission. Now, have a seat. You have a plane to catch in forty five minutes."

"This debriefing shouldn't take no more than ten," Myra said.

Major Jennings turned on the recorder that was on his desk. "State your name for the record."

"I'm known as Myra Taft."

"In your own words, please give a detailed account of your mission."

Myra gave a detailed account of Zakawi's torture techniques and his brainwashing program. She recounted the night she realized that she was being watched. At first she thought it was Army, but then one night when she was in a neighborhood bar she spotted Jamilah. Although she was disguised, Myra knew beyond a shadow of a doubt it was her.

Under the orders of Major Jennings, she allowed herself to be watched, hoping that someone would soon approach her. Soon she was approached, but it was by a low-level drug dealer who, unbeknown to him, was getting his heroin from one of Zakawi's connects in America. Myra knew why Jamilah sent him at her. Myra knew she had to become a heroin user. It was logical that someone with Post Traumatic Stress Disorder would jump at the chance to escape their problems.

Major Jennings interjected. "So, the woman we know as Myra Taft was just a deep cover you created to pinpoint all those involved in this terrorist plot?"

"Yes," Myra responded.

"So you're not addicted to heroin and you don't suffer from Post- Traumatic Stress Disorder."

"Of course not."

Myra went on to give a detailed account of the botched drug sale gone bad and how she had to do what she had to do in order to maintain her cover. Everything from killing the would-be robbers to shooting the police officers who she clearly saw had on bulletproof vests.

When Myra finished giving her account, Major Jennings turned off his recorder. "I don't have to tell you that you guys did an excellent job. I didn't expect anything less. And it was a pleasure to work a mission with you guys. It's been decades since I last worked in the field."

"I don't know why Cleary, Walker, and I agreed to let you onboard. I don't know what we were thinking. If that bullet was a centimeter to the left…"

"Aw, you were really concerned, weren't you?"

"Can I go? I have a plane to catch."

Major Jennings looked at her for a moment.

"What?" Myra said.

"How are you, Myra, really?"

"I fine."

"That's funny. You, Cleary, and Walker are always fine."

"Since when is there something wrong with being fine?"

"What you guys do isn't normal. You guys literally create a character and then become them. With all the characters that you've lived as, it's a miracle that you haven't lost your true identity. It's a miracle that you're still sane. No soldier has ever been rescued from one of Zakawi's camps and has been the same."

"We done?" Myra asked, as she held her hand out.

Major Jennings reached into his pocket and pulled out an envelope containing a birth certificate, social security card, driver's license, passport, credit cards, and a bank account number. Myra took the envelope from him and pulled out the passport.

"Marlene Taft? Really?"

"You're the one who wants first names that start with the letter M.

The pickings are getting slim. Besides, you know it's only temporary. Now if I'm not mistaken, you have a plane to catch to Los Angeles where you'll be enjoying a well-deserved vacation on Uncle Sam's dime."

"See you when I see you, old man."

Major Jennings knew that was Myra's way of telling him what she really couldn't tell him. "I love you, too," he responds.

Diana, Iraq located in Northern Iraq with a population of 125,000; a Muslim woman in full garb enters a mosque and walks into the women's bathroom. "Hello, Sister Maryam." The Muslim sister who's already in there washing her hands greets her.

Baghdad, 9:30 am, a Muslim sister enters a nursery school looking for Jaffar, the Muslim brother who teaches the recitation of the Holy Quran. "As-Salamu alaykum, sister," Jaffar greets her as she approaches him.

Panjshīr, Afghanistan, 11:00 pm, a Muslim woman discreetly knocks on the backdoor of a closed restaurant where she's meeting a man for a secret rendezvous. The man let's her in. "As-Salamu alaykum." Before the woman can greet him back, he's already groping her and sticking his tongue in her mouth.

Sana'a, Yemen, two Muslim newlyweds are enjoying a picnic just outside the city limits. "I love you," the husband says to his wife."

"I love you, too," she responds lovingly.

In the caves along the mountainsides of Iraq, Specialist Myra Taft lies in a dark cave, stretched across a rock, shackled, helpless. It's nighttime; the cold desert temperature has her teeth and bones chattering. The night watchmen gather around her. In spite of the dried feces and urine spread across her skeletal frame, the night watchmen still take their frustrations out on her.

All four women are in sync. Maryam walks up to the Muslim sister performing ablution and in two swift moves, punches her in the throat and snaps her neck.

The Muslim woman in Baghdad allows a dagger to slide from the folds of her sleeve to the palm of her hand. Jaffar doesn't understand what's happening until the woman throws the dagger and it lodges in his throat.

The Muslim woman in Panjshīr allows the man to suck on her neck and reach inside of her dress to cup her breast while she reaches for the 6 inch, stainless steel hairpin used to keep her hair in a bun. In two fluid motions, she pulls his head back and jams the pin through his eye socket and into his brain, causing immediate paralysis and imminent death.

The newlyweds in Sana'a share a kiss.

"Close your eyes," the wife whispers.

The husband obeys with a smile on his face. "You know I don't like surprises."

"Well, you're really not going to like this one," the woman says in perfect English, causing the husband's eyes to pop open in shock. The wife places the .22 silencer to his head.

All of the targets had one thing in common. All were leaders of terrorist cells that were actively recruiting young men and women to carry out terrorist attacks on the U.S.

And all of the women had one thing in common.

"Aminah," the husband says to his wife who's holding a gun to his head. "I don't understand."

"And you never will." She pulls the trigger.

Myra jumps out of her bed and stumbles and then falls against the bedroom wall. She grabs her head and screams. She quickly covers her mouth with both hands and bites down on her fingers to muffle the screams and cries. It takes her a few minutes to blink away the memories, the missions, and the assassinations.

She looks over at the night table and sees *her* prescription for PTSD. She smiles and reaches for the bag of heroin. One of the beauties of having to play a heroin addict was being able to hide the fact that she really was a heroin addict. Nothing else could help her cope with the atrocities she had endured in the name of freedom. Myra was the epitome of a slogan that we always hear but seldom understand: FREEDOM ISN'T FREE.

BY AUTHORS : ALI & ARLENE BRATHWAITE

BRATHWAITE
PUBLISHING